VALLEY OF LIGHTS

Phoenix Police Sergeant Alex Volchak is having a
hard enough time holding together the somewhat
battered remains of his life even before the call to
the Paradise motel. It is at this sleazy location that
he finds the bodies – inert and barely clinging to
life – that the local press are quick to label
'zombies'. And when one of them seems to have got
up from a hospital bed and simply walked away,
Volchak has a major problem on his hands. It is a
problem, furthermore, which no-one else seems
anxious to share, even when Alex becomes
convinced that the incident is related to a gruesome
set of murders.

With masterful skill, Stephen Gallagher moves his
novel from wry police-procedural towards a
terrifying horror story. Before long Alex Volchak
realises that he is involved in a personal struggle
with an almost unimaginable evil. In this struggle,
Alex must win, or die. Or worse . . .

About the Author

Stephen Gallagher is married with a daughter and lives in North Lancashire's Ribble Valley. He is the author of CHIMERA, FOLLOWER and a number of short stories. VALLEY OF LIGHTS marks him as one of the most exciting young writers in this field.

Valley of Lights

Stephen Gallagher

NEW ENGLISH LIBRARY
Hodder and Stoughton

For Ellen

Copyright © 1987 by
Stephen Gallagher

First published in Great Britain in 1987 by New English Library

New English Library Paperback edition 1988
Second impression 1988

Printed and bound in Great Britain for Hodder and Stoughton Paperbacks, a division of Hodder and Stoughton Ltd., Mill Road, Dunton Green, Sevenoaks, Kent TN13 2YA.
(Editorial Office: 47 Bedford Square, London WC1B 3DP) by
Cox & Wyman Ltd., Reading.

British Library C.I.P.

Gallagher, Steve
  Valley of lights.
  I. Title
  823'.914[F]   PR6057.A3895

ISBN 0-450-42268-2

PART ONE

The Shell Game

I was within two blocks' drive of Paradise when the call came over the air. It was a 927, a general code meaning to investigate unknown trouble. The despatch girl was offering it to Travis and Leonard, both of whom were checking IDs for warrants in the scrubby little park around the Adult Center on Jefferson; knowing that I could have them as backup in three minutes or less if the 'unknown trouble' turned out to be something bigger than anticipated, I cut in and took the call. Squad Sergeant responding, one minute or less.

The Paradise Motor Court was one of those places that could make a weekend break at the Bates Motel look halfway attractive. It was on the fringe of that section of Phoenix known as The Deuce, an area of old warehouses and railyards which they reckon got its name during the war from the two-dollar tricks on offer around the streets. I'd first been thrown in there some twelve years before, fresh out of the Academy with my Police Officer 1 grade, and I'd found it to be shabby and scary and inexplicably exciting. As Skid Rows went it hadn't grown any prettier, but my main thought as I pulled onto the Paradise forecourt was to wonder whether the 927 was going to bring me any surprises. I could usually count on a couple of surprises on a good day, even now; some were welcome, some less so.

The clerk was outside and waiting for me, waiting to flag me down. He wore a Hawaiian shirt that was both too large and too loud for him, and he was hopping around like he'd been wired to a battery.

"Sergeant Volchak," I said. "What's the problem?"

"Something here you ought to see," he said. "But come and listen to this, first."

He disappeared into his office, and I followed him. I had

a vague memory of the place from when it had been called something else, but nothing clicked. He was already behind the counter as I came through the door, lifting the handset from the twenty-line switchboard and holding it out to me. One of the board lights was on, but I could see that the key wasn't down. I took the handset and listened, holding it close to my ear but not touching.

I could hear breathing, hoarse and difficult. Nothing else. It sounded like someone sleeping off a long, rowdy drunk. I looked at the clerk, who was wiping his hands nervously on his trousers, and said, "You've tried calling?"

"I've tried calling, I've tried knocking. Nothing works, it's like they're all deaf."

"They?"

"Come on, I'll show you."

And then he was moving again, quick and jittery like before, dodging around me as if he was afraid I might grab him. I left the handset on the desk, and went out again into the hot desert air with its taints of asphalt and auto fumes. The steady drone of the Maricopa Freeway in the middle distance was almost being drowned out by a ghetto-blaster playing loud Donna Summer in the first of the units; windows open, screens unbolted, it was obvious that the Paradise didn't run to air conditioning. Even through the music I heard a panicky scramble as I passed by and the people inside caught a glimpse of the uniform. Give it about five seconds, I was thinking, and then somebody's stash would be making a fast trip down the toilet.

I'd also remembered the last time I was here. It had been about two years into my service; a local prostitute had been found in one of the rooms, stripped naked and strangled on the bed. She'd had what appeared to be two pieces of cotton wool, one placed neatly on each breast; closer inspection showed that her nipples had been clipped off with shears, and the cotton wool was the breast tissue protruding through. It was something so unusual that the ten of us on the squad shift had all invented excuses to call by and take a look, one team at a time, until the shift commander had put a stop to it. I'd begun to wonder if the desk clerk was going to lead me down to the same unit, but then I realised that we'd already passed it. Whatever he was going to show me, I doubted that it was going to be as unusual as what I'd seen on that last visit.

Just goes to prove how wrong you can be, doesn't it?

"I'm new at this," he said back over his shoulder as we turned the corner by a defunct-looking Pepsi machine. "I need somebody to tell me what to do."

"What about the owner?"

"I don't even know who the owner *is*. I've got an emergency number, but nobody's answering."

I tried to reassure him. "Whatever's going on," I said, "I'm telling you, it's not the strangest thing you're likely to come across in this business."

He looked at me bleakly. "Don't bet on it," he said.

We came to the last of the units. Beyond this was some empty parking space and then a high cinderblock wall topped with wire. Not a place, on the whole, that I'd have cared to spend any time in. The desk clerk stood out front and gestured me towards the window as if to say take it, I don't want it, the responsibility's all yours. I was aware that, some distance behind me, one or two people had emerged and were watching to see if anything interesting was going to happen. I stepped up to the window and looked inside.

The sash was open an inch at the top, and some faint stirring of the air had caused the drawn curtains to part down the middle. The bug screen and the darkness inside made it difficult to see anything at all, but as my eyes adjusted I began to make out shapes. Something that had at first looked like a bean bag resolved itself into a human form, slumped halfway out of a low chair as if he'd fainted while sitting. The details weren't clear, but also in my line of sight across the room was the end of the bed with somebody lying on it. I could see a pair of soiled tennis shoes for this one, not much more.

Just drunks sleeping off a party, I thought, remembering the heavy breathing that was being picked up by the dislodged phone, and I turned to the clerk and said, "Who's the room registered to?"

"A little s . . ." he began, but then he caught himself. "A Hispanic guy. I don't think he's even one of them."

11

"Well . . . all I see is people sleeping. I don't know what's so unusual in that."

"For four straight days? It could have been longer. He registered weeks ago, he closed the drapes on day one and he musta sneaked the others in when no-one was watching."

"What about the maid?"

"We're residential, maid service comes extra. She just leaves the towels and sheets outside, doesn't go in. What do you think?"

I felt a definite stirring of interest. I said, "I think you should get your passkey so we can go inside and find out what the problem is."

"And that's legal? I mean, I'm all square with the owner if I do what you say?"

"Get the key, all right?"

We went inside; or rather, I went inside and the little monkey in the technicolor shirt hovered in the doorway behind me. My first expectation, which was of the smell of opium smoke, turned out to be wrong; what hit me instead was a rank odour like bad breath and drains. I crossed the room and opened the window as wide as it would go, and then I turned to look at the place in the harsh angles of daylight.

Nobody had moved. There were three of them. Slumped in the low chair opposite the window was a man in a gray business suit, an expensive-looking summer lightweight with the pants stained dark where his bladder had let go. He was the one who'd fallen against the phone and dislodged the receiver, as if he'd been propped awkwardly and hadn't stayed that way. The soiled tennis shoes on the bed turned out to belong to a short, muscular-looking man in his late thirties, while over in the other chair by the key-operated TV sprawled a black teenager in a leather jacket.

All three of them were inert, like corpses; but I checked for a pulse on each one, and they were all alive and steady. The arms of the man on the bed, who was wearing a T-shirt, showed no fresh needle marks or even old scars.

I said to the clerk, "Did you move anything when you came in before?"

His face was that of an animal that had just been stunned prior to slaughtering. Perhaps he thought I'd read his mind; he probably didn't realise that he'd already given himself away.

"No," he finally managed. "I didn't move a thing." And then; "Is it drugs?"

"I don't know. How do I phone out from here?"

"I have to connect you at the board," he said, almost gratefully, and promptly disappeared.

I eased the receiver out from under the man in the gray summer suit, and replaced it. He didn't react. I gently hauled him upright, and his breathing became better; I was also able to reach into his jacket now and take out his wallet, which proved to be empty apart from half a dozen credit cards which were all in different names and some of which were as much as two years out of date. Putting the wallet back – and fighting the gag reaction at the closeup odour – I noted that his skin was pale and almost translucent-looking, the way skin can go if it's kept in a cast or under a bandage for too long. It reminded me of worm flesh.

The phone gave a single ring, and I picked it up. "Okay," the desk monkey said, "just go ahead and dial," so I did.

"And don't listen," I said as it was ringing out at the other end of the line, and I heard him hurriedly hang up before I got through.

I requested ambulances, and also for a message to be passed along to the narcotics bureau. Something like this, I didn't see how it could be anything other than a drugs-related matter, although I'd no idea what kind of jag could produce this kind of total inertia. The three of them looked wasted, as if they'd been like this for ages; the black kid even looked as if he'd lost weight inside his clothes.

And that was something else, I thought as I went outside to wait in air that was a little fresher. The three of them made a weird set; the only thing that they appeared to have in common was that they had nothing in common. A middle-class businessman, a sharp young black, and a white manual worker, probably unskilled. I had that cop buzz going in my mind, the feeling that I get sometimes

13

when I think I've seen everything and then I run up against something new.

The narcs got there before anybody else, screaming into the court in their confiscated white Porsche and doing a sliding stop on the gravel. They hopped out, leaving the doors wide open; Morrell and McKay, I knew them both slightly. To look at them you'd guess that, if they hadn't grown up to be drug cops, they'd probably have become users instead. Morrell wore an ear-ring, and was first inside; McKay stopped long enough to tell me that their sniffer dog had gobbled up the merchandise in the last dealer's apartment that they'd searched, had ruined their case against the man, and had put itself out of action for more than a week. Lieutenant Michaels, my shift commander, arrived in his unmarked white St Regis a couple of minutes after that, and as I was bringing him up to date the first of the ambulances finally made it and the forecourt *really* began to look busy. Lieutenant Michaels went inside, and I went over to the crowd of about six that had gathered and said, "Okay, go about your business, this isn't a zoo," and everybody moved back maybe a foot. The desk monkey pushed his way through with the registration card for the unit; *Gilbert Mercado*, the signature read. He'd paid up once a week, in advance, and in cash.

Five weeks.

Morrell and Lieutenant Michaels had to come out so that the paramedics could get in with a stretcher. The lieutenant was shaking his head and saying, "I never saw anybody so stoned."

"Stoned?" Morrell said. He was looking considerably paler than when he'd gone in. "Those guys are practically comatose. I started to turn one of them over and he just stopped breathing. Scared the shit out of me, just like he'd died. Then when I rolled him on his back, he started up again. What could do that to someone?"

"You're supposed to tell *us*."

Morrell looked around at the logjam of official vehicles that was now blocking the court, and said, "Well, as soon as the circus here gets out of the way, me and McKay are going to wait inside for the tenant."

"You better," one of the paramedics said as he emerged

14

with the front end of the stretcher. I could see straight away that they'd taken the man from the bed first, because his tennis shoes were the first part of him to emerge. "Because these birds are all done singin'."

That's what always gets me about paramedics; they turn up as jaunty as anything even at the worst carnage, and the whole subtext of their manner is that *Your bad news is our good business*.

Morrell said, "That's your expert opinion, doctor?" Laying heavy on the *doctor*.

"I know brain-dead when I see it," the paramedic said, unfazed. "I'd a thought even a detective would recognise his own kind."

They were only going to be able to get two of them in the one ambulance, but there was another on call. If that came in the next couple of minutes then the court was going to get even more crowded. Lieutenant Michaels came over and said, "You want to leave it with me now, Alex?"

"Sure," I said. I'd been there for more than half an hour already, and I had a squad to check on.

I was almost at the corner with the rusted Pepsi machine when I heard the desk monkey shout from behind me, "Hey, that's him! That's Mercado!" I looked up and found myself face-to-face with a small Mexican-looking guy who was just coming around the corner the other way. He was wearing an army-surplus green T-shirt and a baseball cap, and he was carrying a brown paper sack of groceries. He seemed strong and compact, someone who probably took regular exercise; he spent maybe a second looking at my uniform and then at the scene behind me, and then he simply dropped the sack and ran. He was out of sight even before the sack had hit the ground.

Me, I can't move so fast. I've got strength, but I'm not light on my feet. Mercado was like a bullet. He was out of the court and into the street before I was even halfway to my car, and I knew that if I didn't get wheels under me then I had no chance of ever catching him. I was in the car and rolling, making the tight turn towards the street; and then in the next moment I was standing hard on the brakes as the second ambulance swung in and blocked my way, and we narrowly missed tangling radiators as we stopped nose-to-nose with less than a foot to spare.

I popped the siren and the ambulance backed off, leaving me a clear run to the street, but I knew that I was already too late. Phoenix is mostly a city of wide roads and open spaces where a runner or even a walker is something unusual and easy to spot, but none of that applied in the Deuce. I cruised out into the hot afternoon sun and made a circuit of the block, but Mercado had been swallowed up somewhere in the maze of side-roads and warehouse alleys. There was no point in stopping and asking for witnesses; everyone, I knew, would have been looking somewhere else.

I drove back to the Paradise, calling in a description on the way but not expecting much to come of it. There was one significant detail that put a little hope into the action, however; Mercado was going to find it very hard to disguise the fact that he'd taken a serious beating sometime in the last few days. One side of his face around his eye had been swollen so much that the skin had seemed to be ready to split over his cheekbone. Fast as he was, somebody had been faster.

Morrell and McKay were crouching over the busted grocery sack when I got there, taking samples from the broken jars and knotting them into little plastic bags. As far as I could see, the jars were all of some kind of baby food.

"Jesus," Morrell said as he scrabbled around in the dirt, "look at me. My mother thinks I spend all day being a hero."

Lieutenant Michaels, who was standing over them and watching, said, "How can babies eat that shit? No wonder they cry all the time."

"You find anything?" I said, but the lieutenant shook his head.

"Nothing you could recognise. Maybe the lab'll find something."

"I don't think so," Morrell said from down at ground level. "This is just goo-goo food. None of the jar seals is even broken."

I looked at the split sack again. It was just a mass of glass shards and colored pulp, like some smashed crystal insect

16

with its insides all oozing out. Chocolate, peach, apple and banana.

"So," I said, "we got a mystery?"

"We got a mystery," the lieutenant agreed.

Travis and Leonard were still taking IDs when I caught up with them in the park, and they didn't exactly look as if they were loving every minute of it. It's dull, haphazard work, but sometimes it can throw up a result; closeness to the freight lines and the Plasma Center and the Salvation Army building gives the area a heavy turnover of transients, and random ID samplings have even been known to turn up outstanding homicide warrants in the past. Leonard was off somewhere on the phone to the headquarters computer room, and Travis was standing by their car chatting easily to the people who were waiting for their cards to be returned. One of them, an Indian girl named Maria whom I'd seen around a few times before, was offering to inlay Travis's belt buckle with turquoise. The three young men with her said that they were going over to the employment office to get their cards endorsed so that they could get jobs in Mesa . . . picking fruit, anything. Travis was staying quiet and letting them talk; friendly, but not forward.

I asked, but nobody knew any Gilbert Mercado. Nobody had heard anything about a man of his description getting a beating, either. One of the young men started to tell me about an accident he'd seen two days before, a man hit by a state truck and thrown about sixty feet, a hole in his side the size of a thumb and pouring blood. One of the others said, suddenly, "I had a coat ripped off over at the mission," as if the grief of it had only now caught up with him. Their good nature was running down into nervousness as Leonard's absence with their documentation lengthened. The boy who'd seen the accident said that if there was nothing doing in Mesa, perhaps he'd move on down to Tucson and try there.

Leonard came back – nothing outstanding – handed them their cards, and thanked them all. "Hey, Phoenix," I heard one of them saying as they drifted away, "isn't that some kind of a bird?"

I gave Travis and Leonard a quick summary of what had

happened over at the Paradise, and saw their eyes light up with curiosity. Mercado, I said. He might change his name, but he can't hide the fact that somebody's been using his face for football kicking practice. Then Travis took a call for a noise complaint from Encanto Park, some kids with a stereo system staging their own concert on the bandstand, and as they set off up 15th I resumed my circuit of the district and my efforts to get the Mercado name and description a wider circulation.

I pulled in outside the Salvation Army Center, where half a dozen lost-looking men were hanging around the entrance. Rafael, the one that I wanted, was stretched out in the dust on an unmade sidewalk; the wadded shirt that he was using for a pillow was cleaner than the one that he was wearing. One thing you have to understand about the Deuce, it's informal. I told him what I wanted, told him that I wanted it in the grapevine, and then disappeared from in front of his eyes as I heard a call coming through for a 962, possible 963. Five minutes later I was on somebody's front lawn, looking at a Civic with its front end destroyed; two fire trucks and an ambulance were already in attendance, not to mention the ever-present silent crowd and a few small dogs nosing around the wreck. A woman with head injuries had already been taken out; she was probably going to die, and there was a Vehicular Manslaughter charge on the cards depending on the Hit-and-Run squad's report.

This job. Dull, it ain't.

Lieutenant Michaels caught up with me during my donut break at Winchell's.

"You know, Alex," he said, dropping his hat on the table and sitting down across from me, "that ambulance kid was right."

"About what?"

"I just heard back from the hospital. You know one of them died as they were being admitted?"

"No kidding. Which one?"

"The black kid. They were transferring him to a gurney, and suddenly he wasn't breathing. Anyway, they've run brain scans on the other two, and they didn't find a thing."

I was thinking of what Morrell had said; *I started to turn*

18

him over . . . scared the shit out of me, just like he'd died.
"Both the same?" I said.

"They kicked the plug and they spat on the electrodes, but it still came out as flat as a fart. How about that?"

"Any indication why?"

"Narcotics found nothing and there's no sign of any abuse or injury on the bodies. It's just like they were . . . I don't know, sleeping till doomsday. The TV people wanted to get shots of them, but the chief's playing it safe in case any relatives come out of the woodwork and decide they want to sue."

"Sue for what?" I said.

"Invasion of privacy, exploiting the disabled, whatever. There's a police artist on it instead."

"Lightnin' Leslie?" I ventured.

"The same."

"Everyone he draws looks like one of the Munsters." Lightnin' Leslie was in traffic division, an amateur artist who'd had one big success and had been coasting on it ever since; his depiction from a rape victim's description had actually led to an arrest. The perpetrator *had* looked like one of the Munsters. Rumor was that he'd painted a portrait of the Chief so awful that it only came out at private parties when it was known for certain that the Chief was out of town.

"Yeah," Michaels said. "They say he's signing his pictures in braille, these days."

2

I wasn't always with the Phoenix PD. First I was in the Marines for three years, mostly home-base stuff apart from a spell that I spent on the Guard in the US Embassy in Paris. I was homesick for most of my stay there; people don't believe that when I tell them, but it's true. When I came back I left the service and got married to Eloise, the girl that I'd been going out with since we were both fifteen, and I put all of my savings into a workshop franchise converting cars to run on hydrogen gas. We struggled for a year and then the franchise people folded, leaving me with a lot of useless equipment that was all paid off and several big loans that weren't. It was a bad time all around. We lost the house that we were buying and had to move into what the sales people called America's Last Affordable Home, what the government called Manufactured Housing, and what the rest of us would call a trailer park. And we seemed to be arguing most of the time, the way you do when money pressures make you feel as if you're ready to burst at every weak little seam and debt stands like a thick wall between you and any kind of future.

Eloise packed her bags and left me, twice. We both knew that it was more a way of letting off steam than anything serious, because how far could she expect to get when I was the only person in a fifteen hundred-mile radius who knew how to put another cylinder in the car? The first time, she came back at around three in the morning when I was pretending to be asleep and we never even mentioned it afterwards. The second time, she tried to cut in on a Mack truck as she was joining the Interstate and misjudged the distance by about a foot. Her heart stopped three times on the way to the hospital. She was operated on for more than five hours and that's how long it took the medical team to decide that she should have been let to die in the ambulance. But by then they'd kept her ticking for so long that they were afraid of a lawsuit if they should just let her go, so then I had to hire lawyers to put pressure on for them to do exactly that, and while the lawyers and the doctors were arguing she just slipped away on her own anyway. I wasn't even with her, I was in somebody's office somewhere. All I'd succeeded in doing was to add legal fees to the medical bills, which may help to explain why ten years later I was still living in the mobile home.

I'd still dream about her, sometimes. In the dream I'd be standing by her bed like I did when it was all over, and suddenly she'd open her eyes and say something like, Wow, Alex wasn't that *close*? And I'd agree that it was, and then I'd take her home. And then I'd wake up from the dream and go and stand under the shower for a while, and then I'd go out and lose myself in the job.

I never meant for police work to become my life, but that seems to be the way that it went. I don't know much else. I *do* know that I'm dull company – I've seen the eyes of enough strangers glazing over at parties as I've talked to them about the service – but what can you do? You're who you are.

I didn't connect my dream to my interest in the events at the Paradise Motel. At least, not at that stage.

At the end of the shift I changed out of my uniform and drove home to the trailer park. I may have made it sound lowlife, but it wasn't. It was a quiet little walled acre out in the east of the city where leveed canals run parallel to the roads and the sense of desert living is still strong. The rent was low and there weren't more than a handful of people on the site who were below retirement age, but this only contrasted with the way I spent my days. A bonus which had come along in the last year was that of living right next door to a good-looking young widow whose nine-year-old daughter seemed determined to get the two of us into bed together. I don't know what they teach them in the schools these days. Or perhaps it's the TV.

It was starting to get dark as I drove home that evening, a dusty pink moon sitting low in a blue-metalled sky. I always like the effect of the lines of red tail-lights around that hour, a kind of rustbucket romance that briefly turns ordinary traffic into some kind of carnival; but what I was thinking about tonight was those three ill-matched bodies lying brain-dead in a motel room but somehow still breathing – just – and about Gilbert Mercado, the champion sprinter with the punchbag face and an armful of baby foods.

He was feeding the corpses, obviously. Somehow keeping them alive at only the most basic level. But why?

Loretta's Renegade wasn't there, and I wondered if she'd be out for the evening. It wasn't so much that her daughter's vigorous campaigning was starting to get to me; the truth was that I was glad to have help. As I said, I don't exactly sparkle in company. I went inside, let up the blinds, and turned on the TV to catch *Eyewitness News*. My sitting room was cool enough for me not to have to switch on the air conditioning, but I left open the door to my covered porch to let any breeze blow through.

A big earthquake in southern Italy; Chicano students at the ASU picketing along with striking citrus farm workers in the valley; two Phoenix hospitals running trials with marijuana as part of their therapy for cancer patients, while down in Pinal County the DPS and the Sheriff's office were celebrating a million-dollar bust over the self-same substance after fourteen months of investigation. And coming up next, the anchorman promised as the inlay behind his shoulder carried a shot of the County General, the medical mystery that has detectives and doctors baffled.

Detectives and doctors. No mention of any sergeants in there, I noted.

It was during the commercial break that I heard Loretta's jeep making the turn in alongside the house, and even before the engine died I heard Georgina run up the three steps to their door. She's only a small child and healthily skinny, but she makes more noise than an elephant charge when she runs. The break ended, and the coverage started; a couple of minutes in, I heard a tap on the porch screen. I shouted that it was open.

Loretta came in, glancing at the TV as if she was wary of interrupting anything important. At that moment they were flashing up Lightin' Leslie's rather freehand interpretations of the one deceased and two surviving subjects, none of which looked like any of the faces that I'd seen earlier in the day. As they cut to a shot of the Paradise, I said to Loretta, "You heard about this?"

"If it's about the three coma people, I heard it on the radio. Did it happen in your area?"

"I was the one who found them."

"Ugh, creepy." She sat down on the edge of the couch to hear the rest. "Just censor the details a little when Georgie puts the pressure on, will you?"

They went on into an interview with Lieutenant Michaels – he hadn't said anything to me about *that* – but my chances of hearing what he had to say took a sudden dive when Georgie came hammering up the porch steps and bounced into the room. Her arrival broke the peace with a similar effect to that of a small hand grenade.

22

"Hi, Alex," she said, "were you the one who found the zombies?"

"I found some sick people, that's all," I said, mindful of Loretta's warning. "Zombies get up and walk, but the ones I found weren't going anywhere."

"Were they in coffins? Or just sort of standing around?"

"Now, listen, kid," Loretta cut in, "you can either button up or die young. Choice?"

Georgie chose to button up. The internal pressure made her almost pop-eyed. I said, "It was nothing, Georgie, honest. No coffins, no zombies. All I did was call out an ambulance."

"I bet," Georgie said, her tone conveying that she didn't believe a word of it and that I was keeping the really interesting details for grown-up talk.

"What did we decide?" Loretta said sternly, and Georgina made a hurricane withdrawal.

The item was winding up now with a description of Gilbert Mercado but, thankfully, no picture. No drugs were found anywhere in the room, no traces in the bodies. Over in the next house I could hear Georgie playing her recorder, almost certainly for my benefit. She was a nice kid, but someday somebody was going to have to break the news to her that she had a tin ear for music. Loretta held a straight face for a while, but then snorted with laughter and had to look down and cover her eyes in embarrassment. As the news gave way to an ad for fast-working tablets for diarrhea – no chalky taste, no large doses – I went over and turned off the set.

"What was the radio coverage like?" I asked Loretta as I turned to her again. She was blowing her nose on a tissue after wiping her eyes; in the distant background, Georgie was still murdering *Amazing Grace*.

"The usual," Loretta managed after a moment. "Two minutes of news followed by an hour of crackpot phone-calls with every wild theory you ever heard of coming around again. Is this going to be big for you, or what?"

"It isn't even going to be a police case, from what I can make out. Why?"

"So," she said carefully, "does that mean you're planning to follow it up in your own time?"

"I'm not going to be following it up at all."

"Well, in that case, I'm under orders from Georgie to ask if you'd like to spend the day with us on Wednesday. That *is* your day off, isn't it?"

Across the way, I heard Georgie's recorder stop dead in the middle of a bar.

"Love to," I said. "Anywhere special?"

"I'll provide the picnic if you'll provide the venue. You know the town better than I do and, I'll be honest, coping with the Katzenjammer Kid over there seems to have ruined my decision-making capability."

Was it my imagination, or could I hear the Katzenjammer Kid jumping around next door and shouting *Yay! Yay!*? I said, "I'll think of something."

Loretta got up to go, but now her face was serious. She lowered her voice, so that it wouldn't carry.

"Listen, Alex," she said. "We both like you a lot. But if this gets to be an embarrassment, you can tell me and . . . we'll stop it there. All right?"

"It hasn't happened yet," I said.

Neither of us moved, but there was either some understanding going back and forth there or I was seriously misreading the signals. Bless the kid, I didn't think I could have come this far without her; I'd have had Loretta stunned and poleaxed with my one-note personality just like all the others, smiling a fixed smile and casting shifty glances around for the nearest exit. We'd come through all that, past the point where first impressions mattered more than anything else. I hadn't got a clue what I was going to say next; Loretta was about to speak, but then Georgie broke the silence again as only Georgie could.

"Have you seen the *time*?" She yelled from the doorway, and then clattered away again.

"You have to go somewhere?" I asked Loretta.

"Would you believe disco classes? For nine-year-olds? And they're not cheap, Alex, believe me."

"I believe it."

"But all the other girls go, so . . ."

"Yeah, I know," I said as I held the screen door open for her. "It used to be ballet."

"Not any more," she said. "Not enough pizazz in the accessories."

I heard them going out again in the jeep, five minutes later. I didn't know the exact nature of Loretta's financial problems, but I did know from the odd remark she'd dropped that her late husband had been somewhere around my own league as a business genius. She was training now as a window dresser in one of the big mall stores somewhere over in Scottsdale; her supervisor was a nineteen-year-old kid who was, from all accounts, a complete and utter jerk who thought it was quite a joke to have an older woman as an assistant. We'd had a few barbecues in the summer, and I'd taken her out twice while Georgie stayed home with a sitter. She stood five-five and was dark-haired with blue eyes; it was an unusual combination, and the first thing that had struck me about her.

I turned the TV on again and ran through the channels, but I couldn't find anything to hold my attention. Everywhere seemed to be running cop shows except for Trinity, where a middle-aged pansy with a fluffball haircut was talking about snatching the land out of the devil's hands.

So then I took out the trash, keeping a wary eye open for Mrs Moynahan and her notebook full of real and imaginary misdemeanors observed about the site, and all the time my mind was running around and around in the same circle. Mercado and the zombies, the zombies and Mercado.

Then I sat and tried to think of somewhere that a nine-year-old might like to visit on the coming Wednesday, but still it was the same.

I'd told Loretta that I wasn't going to be doing anything about this on my own time.

And I wasn't, of course.

3

Of anywhere in the city, Produce Alley is probably the first area to come alive in the mornings. It's a low-rise zone of warehouses and sheds close to the freight tracks, and in the hours before dawn all of its doorways and shady corners fill up with people in thick jackets and baseball caps who squat with their bundles and wait for the citrus trucks to come in. The trucks unload their boxes and then, if the waiting hopefuls are in luck, they'll load up again with documented workers who are prepared to go out to the valley farms as cheap non-union labor. Mostly Chicanos, the workers can look forward to a few weeks of fruit-picking as they live either in dormitories or in makeshift camps.

I hadn't been able to sleep. This was a long shot, I knew, but it had occurred to me that this was one possible way that Mercado might make his way out of the city in darkness without either getting his hands on a car or showing his battered face at a ticket window.

The pavement was still wet in patches from last night's hosing-down; right now it was sharp and cold, a chill that would vanish into the dusty heat of the coming morning. I was out of uniform and in my own car, and nobody paid me much attention as I cruised slowly by and tried to make out faces in the gloom. I didn't have much chance of seeing detail, but what I had in mind was the application of what an old sergeant of mine had called the 'Heat Factor'; he mostly applied it to people in cars, zooming up close behind them and staying tight on their tails to see if guilt would provoke them into some kind of panic reaction. Most of what I was getting back here was no reaction at all, until I came around by a row of what looked like shutter-fronted garages with big zinc garbage hoppers alongside. As I slowed and stared, I saw somebody giving me a half-hearted wave.

It was Rafael, my so-called informant who had rarely given me much more than promises. He was grinning and shivering as I stopped the car and got out, and the people around and behind him seemed to fade back into the shadows as I walked over.

"What's this, Sergeant Volchak," he said, "you moon-lighting now?"

"Couldn't sleep," I said. The first streaks of the dawn were beginning to tear up the sky over in the East beyond the tower of the Hyatt Hotel, and the people in the alley began to rise like prairie dogs as the sounds of truck engines came through the still air. I said, "I'm still looking for a line on Gilbert Mercado."

Some people were starting to move, others were staying where they felt their chances were better. Rafael said, "How'd you know I'd be here?"

"I didn't. But I thought *he* might be. Have you heard anything?"

"Honest to God, Sergeant Volchak, it's a big city." Rafael gave a nervous glance as a big six-wheeler made the turn into the alley, with another one close behind; their sound rattled the shutters on either side, forcing him to shout. "If you people don't know what's going on, who does?"

"Okay," I said. "Just don't forget that I asked."

"Please, Sergeant. I'm missing all my chances here."

I let him go, and had to move my car so that the trucks could get by. The first one made a show of almost scraping me for getting in the way in the first place; I couldn't see any driver up there, just this big metal monster that could easily have been rolling along on its own dim intelligence with nobody in the cab. I briefly thought about getting out my badge and giving him a hard time, but I let it go. Back in the old days I wouldn't even have hesitated, but the satisfaction goes out of it.

Instead I got out again and walked around, looking more closely at faces now that the light was starting to cut contrasted areas out of the gloom. More trucks were arriving and would-be workers were scrambling around them to help with the unloading and so, they hoped, improve their chances. The turnover would be fast, and by nine the Alley would be fully daylit and close to dead again, its main business already over. I walked along the rows, my hands stuck deep into my windcheater pockets, feeling the chill. They say that your blood thins in this kind of climate. Takes a couple of years if you come from somewhere cooler, but then anything below seventy degrees has you reaching for a sweater.

I'll be honest, I was starting to lose interest. I was circling back towards my car and ready to go home or to find an all-night place for some breakfast when a figure broke out from the shadows in front of me and started to run. I couldn't see his face, but his size and his speed instantly said *Mercado*; and I started forward, cursing myself for my slow reaction and my loss of faith in my own obviously godlike powers of deduction.

He was dressed like all the others – that is, much as he'd been yesterday with a jacket added – and if he'd kept his head down I expect that I'd simply have walked on by without even noticing him. I don't think a rat could have scampered down the alley as fast as he did; I was doing my best, but I could already see that it wasn't going to be good enough. He jumped some boxes, elbowed some people out of the way, and squeezed down by the side of one vehicle to get out the other side and into the wider access road. I slammed through after him, and gained a couple of yards; he'd skidded on some dumped skins in the gutter, but he hadn't stopped and he'd picked up his balance again as he ran.

There were more people out here, and more illumination from head and tail-lights as business hit its noisy peak. The Alley was transformed, like a graveyard that had suddenly pulled its covers away to reveal some coarse and brutish fairground. Nobody tried to stop Mercado or to interfere with him, or with me; they simply moved aside when they saw us coming and probably looked after us when we'd passed, a common piece of street theater with some curiosity value.

We'd covered maybe two hundred yards and I was doing better than I'd expected, holding the distance even if I wasn't gaining any. Mercado had looked back once, and it had cost him time. Now, as a wagon swung out ahead of him with a number of shapes huddled under the canvas in the load area behind, I saw him put on a spurt.

He was going to try to get aboard, before the wagon picked up speed and got out onto the main street. I was close to being finished, but he didn't know that. I saw him take three long steps, and then jump; he caught the edge of the tailboard and quickly brought his legs up, hanging on tight and kicking around for a foothold.

I couldn't swear to what happened next. The wagon was making the turn and I was slowing down, knowing that I had no chance of catching it and wondering if I'd even be able to get my car out of the market in time to follow. Mercado had got himself a foothold in what looked like the loop of chain from the tailboard pin, and he was struggling up and over when suddenly the tailboard slammed down and Mercado went with it.

My first fear was that he'd bounced on his head; on hard pavement, that's never a good sign. But almost immediately he was making weak moves to raise himself up, and my guess was that he was probably stunned or winded. The truck had stopped about fifty yards further on; someone in the back might have knocked on the cab, but it was more likely that the driver would have heard the tailgate's fall. It was possible that Mercado, kicking around with his foothold on the chain, might have jerked out the pin. Then perhaps his weight had sheared the second pin, or maybe there hadn't even *been* a second pin. It was an old-looking vehicle, well-used.

There was another possibility, that of somebody already on board giving him a little help. I looked over toward the truck as I reached Mercado, and a dozen blank faces stared back. I knew the answer before I even had to ask the question. Nobody saw anything.

Mercado was still struggling to rise, and I crouched down beside him and helped him to sit about halfway up. That seemed to be all that he could manage for the moment in his winded state, which meant that I had to stay where I was and support him. As long as he didn't cry out or start spitting frothy blood from deep in his lungs I was hardly likely to be complicating any breakages. He seemed to have lost his sense of place for the moment, and needed to see where he was to get his bearings again.

Let me explain that I wasn't feeling too good about all of this. I said, "You're not in any trouble. Why did you run?" And his eyes came around to my face and focussed on me hard, as if seeing me before had meant nothing but now he was looking with an intention to remember. He tried to speak normally, but there was so little breath in him yet that it came out no louder than a whisper.

He said, "I don't like questions."

"I only wanted to ask you what happened back there at the Paradise."

"Well," he said, "now you'll never know."

And then he did the weirdest damned thing I'd ever seen. He simpled rolled up his eyes and died on me.

My arm was under his shoulders and I could almost swear that I could feel the life flood out of him all in a rush; but still it was several seconds before I fully understood what had happened, and it was with disbelief that I lowered his sagging weight and felt by his throat for a pulse. There was nothing.

I'd seen people die before. Not many, but in my line of work it's inevitable. I'd never seen anybody go like Mercado did; he was suddenly an empty glove, a discarded thing.

And this was the tough part to accept – he'd shown every sign of doing it deliberately.

I laid him flat and closed his eyes, and then I pulled somebody out of the crowd and told him to find a phone. A fatal accident with an off-duty officer in attendance, I told the man, and then I made him repeat it. By the time that I turned to look at Mercado again I think that I'd more or less rewritten the last few minutes in my own mind, giving myself a set of reactions that I could more easily live with.

The crowd didn't last as long as most; these people were here to catch a job, and watching was getting them nowhere. They'd mostly drifted away and I was into an argument with the truck driver as to why he couldn't do the same, since he was at the other end of the vehicle and facing the other way and hadn't actually *seen* anything, when no less than six night-shift PD cars with their howlers running appeared like banshees out of the dawn and converged nose-in on the scene. The driver clammed up fast and was suddenly the soul of co-operation; the reason for the heavy turnout, I found, was that the man I'd sent to the phone had misreported the whole thing as a fatality involving a cop. I decided to be charitable and assume that the expressions on the faces of the various patrols as they climbed back into their units were of relief that I'd been found walking and in one piece; but wasn't there also just a little bit of disappointment that their cavalry charge had led them to nowhere?

My opposite number on the night shift, Bernie Horowitz, radioed in for the ambulance call to be moved down a notch of priority. If it came down to a choice between someone in a serious accident and Mercado, Mercado was the one who'd complain least if he had to wait. Bernie was the same age as me, with a similar length of service; back in the early days he'd tried to persuade everyone to call him 'B.J.', which inevitably meant that he acquired the lifelong nickname of Blowjob Horowitz.

"You see any of this, Alex?" he asked me afterwards.

"I saw it all," I said. "I had the best view of anybody, if you don't include the victim."

He shook his head, at the marvel of it. "A witness with a fixed address," he said. "That's a novelty, on this piece of turf."

Bernie and I stood and chatted for a while as his patrolmen did all the marking and measuring and statement-taking that the book calls for. When the police photographer and the woman from the medical examiner's office had arrived and seen all they wanted, Bernie and I went over and I confirmed my identification. Everybody on the team had heard about the Paradise mystery by now, and they all came around to take a look at the face of the little guy who'd held the key to it.

Nobody was any the wiser for looking.

It was a full hour before the ambulance came to take him away, and we'd covered him with a blanket by then. When they'd backed it in and the paramedic came around to open the doors, I said, "Are you the only ambulance in this city, or what?"

"The only *good* one," he said, and then he looked at me again. "Didn't I see you in uniform yesterday?"

"My other life," I said.

"Well, here's something you won't know. We just came over from County General and the place is like, unbelievable. They've got the big guys stalking through the corridors looking for little guys to nail to the wall, and out in the parking lot you've got to zigzag to avoid the malpractice lawyers scrambling out of cars in their pyjamas."

"For what?"

"All because one of the zombies walked."

"Say again?"

"It happened about an hour ago. One of them died, right? Just quit breathing in the Emergency Room when a couple of nurses turned him over. Well, one of the others decided that he disagreed with the doctor's diagnosis. He got out of bed, helped himself to somebody's clothes, and then walked out.''

"Did anyone actually *see* him?"

"Two witnesses, one of them a Reverend in for minor surgery. Said it restored his faith in the resurrection.''

If there was a witness, then it could hardly have been body-snatching. I've heard of weirder things.

The paramedic added, as they brought out the folding stretcher for Mercado, "I'd have liked to have seen it myself. Yesterday I'd have laid a bet with anyone. Between the ears, those guys were just dead meat.''

4

A wrong diagnosis. What else could it have been? They say that in most things you tend to get the results that you're looking for if you don't walk in with an open mind. Machines could be faulty, tests could be rushed, maybe there was a slapdash intern on the case who couldn't be bothered to wait around long enough for the little bumps and curves on the screen that meant *somebody home*.

You can see why it intrigued me. I was used to the bizarre . . . but bizarre things in sequence, that was something else. I'd been the first one in the room at the Paradise, and mine had probably been the last face that Gilbert Mercado had seen before he dashed to his death; I was closer to it than just about anybody else, but when I looked around me I couldn't see anything that made logical sense.

I found a place for breakfast, a Denny's twenty-four hour diner some way further down Van Buren. A tall youth in glasses and a dishwasher's apron was wiping down the counter as I went in, and the three men already sitting there were all turned to watch him as if he was putting on the most interesting show of the early morning.

As I waited for my order, I tried to think of somewhere

that I could take Loretta and Georgie on the Wednesday. That would be tomorrow, I realised with a faint sense of shock; I tended to orient myself by my shift pattern rather than by the days of the week, and the regular order of things had become a little scrambled when I'd filled in for one of the other sergeants on my last two rostered days off. I could take them to the zoo in Papago Park, I decided. This decision wasn't entirely uninfluenced by the fact that I'd been given some guest passes by Frank, one of the assistant managers there, when I'd gone out on a call about a deer that had been running loose on the highway not too far from where I was sitting now. Three kids had let the deer out of the petting area and it had run out through a delivery gate; someone in a passing pickup shot the deer on the move and then drove on, we never found out who.

Okay, the zoo. Now, how was I going to get any closer to the explanation of Mercado and his weird, walking, brain-dead menagerie?

The rest of the city had more or less come to life by the time I got to the third floor of the main police building on West Washington. I didn't know many people around here, working as I did out of Sky Harbor station, but I knew Estelle in Information and Records. I'd even been out with her a couple of times, back before she'd been married. She ran me the last week's reports of fights and assaults and, with her knowledge of the new codes and categories, helped me to narrow them down to the two or three that might actually get me somewhere. With fights we get a lot of uncompleted calls, people ringing in because they want the police to appear and break it up but then not wanting to give their names or get involved; one of these was the one that attracted me most. Working on my own, I might have taken half a day just to get this far. Estelle had me turned around and out again in fifteen minutes.

The call had come from somewhere on the south side of Encanto Park; on my shift, as it happened. Travis and Leonard had responded to a call about a gang of white males pursuing and attacking a male Hispanic – the reporting system's phrasing, not mine – but had found nothing when they got there. They'd probably checked it with me, and I hadn't even remembered.

I got in the car and drove over. I knew the area well; it wasn't cheap, but then in the cheap areas they don't so much report their street fights as gather together and start making bets. Alongside the park the houses were neat and private, pastel shades of brick set well back from the avenues behind unfenced lawns. Housebreakers loved them. I put my uniform jacket on over my street clothes and walked up and down for a while; from here I could see a piece of the park through the trees, dusty sloping grassland running down towards the Kiddieland rides.

It was quiet; eerily so, as if the avenues slept all day and only came alive in the evenings and at weekends. I was about to give up and go back to the car when I saw movement behind a window in one of the houses; two minutes later, there was an old guy waiting at the end of the drive for me. Probably had his own room in his daughter's house, nothing to do all day but watch television. He didn't look as if he moved very well. He leaned on a stick as I walked down towards him, his head tilted slightly as if to get the best line of sight through his glasses. He was about the same age my father would have been, if he'd lived.

There are people like him everywhere, but it takes trust and a little time to draw them out. Once they're in the open, the difficult part is to get them to shut up; he told me everything, his life story included, and somewhere in the middle of it was this little gem of a scene with Gilbert Mercado being chased across the park by a group of assorted men, a couple of them in shirts and ties. They had him down and gave him a leathering, but then he got out from under and ran north up the avenue, cutting across the gardens and out the back so that they lost him.

Shirts and ties? That didn't sound like any gang warfare to me, but the description of Mercado was about right. After I'd managed to prise myself away from my witness, I checked my watch and saw that I had just enough time for one more call before I'd have to get down to Sky Harbor for the start of my shift. I went to St Joseph's Hospital, less than half a mile from the park in the direction in which Mercado had last been seen running.

From what I could remember of his face, I wouldn't have been surprised at a broken cheekbone under all that swelling; not something that anyone could easily shrug off or ignore. The emergency room nurse that I'd been hoping to see wasn't on duty, but one of the others was able to tell me that Mercado hadn't run to them for treatment, and that I wasn't the first one to ask; on the day in question three white males, two of them in shirts and ties and all of them damp and breathless from running, had wanted to know if 'a little spic with a sore head is hiding anywhere around here'. When the intern in charge had asked them to leave and then threatened to call the police if they didn't, they withdrew with a warning that 'he'll need more than a hospital if he comes hanging around the playground again'.

So there it was. Middle-class vigilantes, out to protect their children. I was one step further along, and it was getting even *more* complicated; it was like I was walking into a fog which grew denser and darker instead of clearing.

But the first ray of light was about to arrive.

I was driving back along the park, telling myself that I ought to be leaving the detective work to the detectives, when I saw a big clot of vehicles around the Encanto Boulevard entrance and had to slow as I joined the short tailback. There were several of our vehicles plus the KOOL television news van; the patrolman who was out on the road waving traffic by didn't recognise my car, and I didn't pull in. I'd find out what was happening soon enough. I glimpsed more vehicles in the park itself, and one of our helicopters out of Deer Valley making a low pass over the trees.

Down at Sky Harbor I saw Travis in the parking lot, but he'd only just arrived himself and knew no more than I did. We went in through the side door, supposed to be an exit-only from the gym but a regular shortcut to the locker room used by everybody, and found the place even more crowded than was usual at the changeover of the watch. Attention was focussed right down at the far end of the room, where I could just see a pale face that I recognised as belonging to Vincent Avery, the youngest of our probationary patrolmen. The kid was in shock and didn't even know it, I could read as much from where I was standing. Then somebody moved, and I couldn't see any more.

Bernie Horowitz, in the sergeants' office, said, "You

didn't hear? We got a child torture-murder in Encanto Park. Little kid taken from his house sometime this morning, his mother didn't even know he'd gone until she called him through for lunch. Thought he was quiet because he was reading comic books. Some sicko had taken him out to the park, abused him, and then tried to eat him. Avery and Timms were cruising the park after a noise complaint, somebody down on the bandstand with a ghetto blaster, and some kids flagged them down. That's how they found him. At that stage he was still alive, but he didn't make it. Timms went on home already, but Avery's trying to be tough about it."

"A mistake."

"Tell *him* that. I'm just glad it wasn't me. I've seen most things, but I can't take child abuse."

When I went past the locker room again, I heard Avery saying, too loudly, *I was covering him over while we waited for the ambulance to get there, and he was* thanking *me* . . . I got into uniform and then went up to see if I could find Lieutenant Michaels. He'd come in early and all of the officers were now in some kind of meeting concerning the murder, so I took the spare chair by his desk and waited.

On the other side of the partition wall, I could hear somebody on the phone. *Yeah, I saw the body*, he was saying. *Believe me, you do* not *want to know*.

Damn it, I had something here. I wasn't exactly sure what, but I couldn't wait to tell Dave and see what he thought.

He came through from the meeting a couple of minutes later. He left the office door wide open like he always did, and as he dropped his sheaf of mimeoed notes onto the desk and walked around behind it to sit, he said, "I hear you've got a theory for me."

"Not a theory, Dave," I said, "but it's a line I think we ought to follow."

"Okay," he said. "Fire away."

So then I started to tell him about my morning's work, and after a couple of minutes I was starting to be sorry that I'd even begun. It was like when you try to tell somebody about a dream you had which made perfect sense at the time, but then you can feel that sense slipping away even as you speak. I was okay on Mercado keeping three empty shells in a darkened motel room as he cruised the city's parks and playgrounds, but beyond that everything started to sound very shaky. Michaels stopped scanning his meeting papers as he listened. I hadn't meant it to come out as any kind of a theory, but that's how it was starting to sound; and after another minute or so, he cut in.

"Alex," he said, "we don't have a sequence here. Nobody walked out of the hospital."

"But what about the witnesses?"

"One heavily-doped Reverend and a psychiatric patient who has regular conversations with dead presidents. Are these witnesses you'd care to take into court?"

"I've had worse. What about the stolen clothes?"

"Just another petty theft from the County General. According to the patient's brain scan, he'd no right even to be *breathing*. Can you imagine those doctors being wrong?"

"I can imagine them seeing the proof and then firing a few junior people and saying it was what they'd always suspected," I said. I'd stopped subscribing to the popular view of doctors as gods walking the Earth when I'd butted heads with a group of them ten years before, and Dave knew all about it. He conceded the point with a brief smile, but that was as far as he was prepared to take it.

"Listen," he said, "I think I know why you're doing this. The dead stay dead, Alex. It's about the only damn thing we can be sure of in this world. What we're looking at here is a case of bodysnatching for the usual kind of reason."

The usual kind of reason being the desire of close relatives to avoid identification so that they can't be stiffed for the medical bills . . . something else I knew plenty about. I didn't like the sympathetic streak that had crept into the lieutenant's manner here, and I also didn't like the feeling that I was somehow being managed. I could see that I was on the road to nowhere, and that it was time to let the whole thing go. It was out of my system and I couldn't ask for more than that.

Michaels said, "Look, what you've said is noted. If we get any more and it's enough to be worth passing along to the detective division, I'll do it. But until then, what have we actually got?"

"Nothing," I said, and I stood up to leave.

I was halfway out of the door when something else

occurred to me. I said, "Tomorrow's supposed to be a leave day for me. Is that going to be cancelled now?"

"No," he said, "the manpower side of it's all covered. Stay home and relax, you've done two straight weeks without a break. Don't you have anything fixed?"

"Yeah," I said, remembering. "I'm going on a picnic."

The rest of the day was more or less normal. The detective squad diverted most of its personnel into the new investigation, and the uniforms added extra patrols of parks and playgrounds which were now mostly deserted anyway.

Life went on.

5

"You told a lie," Loretta said to me the next morning.

"When?"

"When you said that you weren't going to spend any of your own time on this. I heard you, when you went out at the crack of dawn yesterday."

I'd been telling her about how I'd almost made myself look like one of those guys who stands on street corners and shouts about the FLYING SAUCERS that are in the sky above us RIGHT NOW and the government knows it but WON'T TELL THE PEOPLE. We'd walked all of the way around the city zoo's three different habitat zones and had finally come to rest on a bench near the birds of prey. School holidays and yesterday's scare had made the zoo a popular place to be, but there was so much of it that it still seemed to be almost deserted. Georgie, with the typical perversity of small children, had paid far less attention to any of the exotic breeds than she was now paying to a tray of day-old chicks in a low shed across the way; she was pressed up against the window, watching them as they milled around like street extras in *Blade Runner*.

I looked at Loretta. She was shading her eyes against the sun, smiling. I said, "I couldn't sleep, that was all."

"I've been watching you, Alex," she said. "You're a workaholic."

"A workaholic wouldn't have made such a hash of the lieutenant's exam."

"I don't mean in that way. But outside of the job, what else do you do?"

"Lots of things," I said uncomfortably. "I've done evening classes. I'm in a couple of clubs."

"The evening classes were in law, and the clubs are rifle clubs."

"I told you that?"

"You did."

"Are you saying that I'm dull company?"

"Not at all. But I'm wondering what I'll have to do to keep your interest. Perhaps if I went out and committed a robbery, then you could catch me and put the cuffs on me."

I feigned surprise. "That the kind of thing you're into?"

"If that's the kind of thing that it takes," she said. The way that the shadow was falling across her eyes, I couldn't see how serious she was being. Perhaps that was deliberate.

Georgie came over then, and said, "Mom, if we get the right kind of eggs, could I try hatching them?"

"And then what, sugar? I don't think Mr Peabody's likely to let us put a hen run in the trailer park."

I could just imagine it; first the hen run, then a few cars up on blocks, then a moonshine still, and then the rest of us sitting out on our porches playing banjos. And in the middle of it all, old Peabody the site manager with his hand clutching at his heart and with his lips barely moving.

I said, "Try suggesting it at school. That way you get all the fun, and somebody else gets all the problems."

"Yeah," Georgie conceded, seeing all of the gleam slowly fade from her plan. "But then they'd be everybody's."

She thought it over a moment longer, and then seemed to sense a new tactical avenue; she said, "How about a cage bird?"

"Maybe someday," Loretta said in that parental tone that really means *maybe never*. "Are you all done, over there? Alex says he's got some other places for us to see."

39

"I'll go say goodbye," Georgie said, and ran off down the unmade path. She was in jeans and sneakers and a cowgirl shirt, and she raised more dust than a dirt bike.

Loretta was shaking her head. "Would you believe it?" she said. "A million dollars' worth of imported wildlife, and the kid goes crazy over a box of ten-cent chicks."

"You going to tell her what they're being bred for?"

"I think she probably knows." Georgie was back at the brooder shed window now, on her toes and looking inside again. "But some things are best if you don't say them out loud."

Amen to that, I thought.

For the picnic and for the afternoon, we went out to the Pioneer open-air museum and wandered around amongst the old and reconstructed buildings. We spread the checkered cloth in some shade by the pond overlooked by John Marion Sears' Victorian mansion, broke out the food, and waited for the ants. Watching Georgie, I couldn't help wondering if she was lonely and if, in some ways, she wasn't having to grow up too fast. I suppose it was the cage bird business that had set me thinking. By the time that I was her age I'd been through just about every kind of animal that walked, crawled or flew, including a big yellow dog that had died of a tumor at five years old. I grew up believing that kids ought to have pets, but Georgie didn't have any. She lived in a place where the nearest person to her in age was her own mother. She had her own house key, kept her own hours, and had more freedom and responsibility now than I'd had when I was fifteen.

But if she was unhappy, none of it showed.

When the day had begun to fade, we headed for home over the mountain road. We came over the crest and there it was, a whole valley of lights against the black velvet of a desert evening, a low-rise city tricked into beauty by a fierce sunset and an unexpected approach. We pulled off for a while and watched as the sky flared through from blood-red to black and the city pulsed with evening traffic. It hadn't been a bad day, if you considered my lack of experience as an entertainments manager.

And it wasn't to end there, because even before we were out of the car Loretta was announcing dinner and I was being pushed back behind the wheel so that I could go and find somewhere to sell me some wine. It was almost five miles down the road to the nearest liquor store – the only one that I could be certain of, anyway – and it took me more than half an hour to complete the round trip with something French that I'd never tried but which looked awfully classy.

I didn't make it entirely unscathed. When I was back at the site and getting out of my car, I heard a voice call, "Sergeant Volchak?" It was a voice that I recognised with a sinking heart.

"Yes, Mrs Moynahan?" I said.

"He was here again." Mrs Moynahan was short and stocky, and always looked as if she was ready to leap to the attack. She lived in the most old-fashioned looking unit on the site, a silver Jetstream like an aluminium bullet. She was coming across the road to me now, mostly a silhouette just slightly warmed by the reflected glow of Loretta's curtains.

I said, "And who was this?"

"The man from the CIA. Snooping around, knocking on everybody's door." She thrust a piece of paper towards me. "I made a list of all the places that he went. This is a copy, you can keep it."

I hesitated, and then took the paper. Where was the harm? I said, "Did you speak to him?"

"No. I pretended I wasn't in. Are you going to . . ?"

"Yeah," I said, "we'll put it all into the police computer. Then when he makes a wrong move, we can grab him."

It was my standard answer, but it was the only thing that ever seemed to satisfy her. Poor old stick. I pushed her piece of paper into my pocket as I went up the wooden steps and into Loretta's house, reflecting that I'd at least escaped without having to listen to the usual half-hour of theories and observations. I can handle these things on the street, but with neighbors you have to approach it differently.

There was no sign of anybody when I got inside. The table wasn't set, apart from two glasses, and there wasn't even a light in the kitchen; but then I heard Loretta, calling to me from somewhere in the back.

"Who were you talking to?" she said.

"Mrs Moynahan, from across the way." I set the bottle

down alongside the glasses. "She gives me reports on everybody who goes by. There's a salesman been calling around for the last week trying to get the whole site to bulk-order its toilet paper, she's got him marked down as a government agent. Where's Georgie?"

"With her friends."

"Running loose? Loretta, I don't think . . ."

"She's not running loose, she's with the Hendersons. The Hendersons have a pool and an Old English Sheepdog and they're having a poolside barbecue for Jilly Henderson's birthday. I drove her there while you were out."

What was this, a conspiracy? Georgie hadn't said anything about it. "Loretta . . ." I began.

"Yes, Alex?" Loretta said patiently.

"Why are we shouting from opposite ends of the house?"

I heard movement, and then a moment later she appeared in the doorway. She was mostly backlit from the bedroom, and she was wrapped in a towel.

As far as I could see – which was quite a lot – she wasn't wearing anything else.

"Damn it, Alex," she said, "is it too much trouble just to come through and get a surprise?"

"Try it without the towel," I suggested, "and I'll tell you if it's worth the walk."

One stunned second later, I was walking.

6

Later on, after the wine and some Mexican food out of Loretta's freezer, Loretta went to pick up her daughter and I walked the half-dozen yards back to my own home. There you go, Georgie, I was thinking; it all worked out the way you wanted, and you weren't even around to know it. I messed around, straightening a few things and moving some unpaid bills from one drawer to another, until I heard them get back.

Even then, I couldn't relax. One of those lights out in the valley stood for a child-killer, a torturer, and I still couldn't shake the feeling that I was almost within reach of some kind of understanding. A light had gone out when Mercado had died but then another, just as surely, had blinked on somewhere else. It was the pattern, the damned pattern, so persuasive that it hardly seemed to matter that it wasn't actually possible.

I pulled my canvas gun roll out from under the bed, and started on the cleaning-and-oiling routine. Hardly realised what I was doing, until I looked down and saw that I was holding the hunting rifle almost as if I was expecting Mercado to appear outside and say, *Hi, Alex, I've come for the kid.*

Was that it? Was I getting all raw and protective because, for the first time in years, it was starting to look as if I had something to protect? Not that my eyes weren't wide-open; I'd noticed without commenting on the picture in Loretta's bedroom that was supposed to be hidden behind a stack of her romance paperbacks, and I'd said nothing to break the long silence afterwards. We'd both been around, we weren't children; but I wanted to think that there was still some of that special innocence in us both, the kind that Georgie showed when she looked at a tray of day-old chicks destined only to survive long enough to be live food for the reptiles and hawks. The kind of innocence that can be lost so easily, like when somebody says the obvious out loud.

Mercado could still come, I was thinking. His body may be in the morgue, but *he's* still out there.

But I couldn't say it.

Not to anybody else.

7

I hit paydirt with my twelfth residential motel, just as I was starting to get weary and to believe that I was taking a long

43

shot that would get me nowhere. Most of the desk monkeys so far had known me already, which had meant that I didn't have to show my badge and risk the trouble that this might cause if ever it got back; but the young man behind the counter at the Sunset Beach Motor Court didn't know me, and I didn't know him. He was tall and skinny and wore glasses and had the air of somebody with an education who hadn't been able to make any good use of it. He was two or three years too old for this job to be any kind of a stop-gap.

I said, "I'd like to see your registration cards for the last couple of days." I showed him my ID as I said it. He seemed to shrink back nervously, as if I was suddenly giving off heat.

"Uh, listen," he said, "let me get the regular manager in on this one. I'm just relief . . ."

"No, *you* listen," I said patiently. "I'm going to start again, and this time we're going to do it right. I'd like to see your registrations for the last couple of days. I'm looking for a white male, alone and without luggage, five-eleven, medium build, dark hair. He's kind of pale and wasted-looking, as if he's been lying around in the dark for a long time." Which, of course, he had; I was describing the body in the business suit that I'd last seen slumped in a Paradise chair with urine stains down its pants, the one that had suddenly upped and walked out of County General within moments of Gilbert Mercado hitting the concrete. One of my details seemed to strike a spark with the clerk, and I said, "You've seen him?"

"Kind of white like a slug?" he said.

"And probably no car. Is he in now?"

"No. He went out."

"When did he arrive?"

He moved down the counter to an indexed carousel. "Mid-evening," he said, starting to check through, "the night before last. Right at the end of my shift." He pulled out a card, and passed it down the counter to me. "He paid cash in advance. I saw a gold American Express card in his wallet, but he didn't use it."

For the simple reason that it had been stolen, I was thinking. He'd taken it, along with most of the rest of a surgery chief's clothing, from a locker in the scrub facility

44

right next to the Operating Rooms. According to the surgeon, he'd have about two hundred and fifty dollars in cash on him. When I heard that, I *knew* I'd taken up the wrong profession.

Bodysnatching, huh?

The card told me nothing; utterly anonymous handwriting, a name I'd never heard of, an out-of-state address that was probably false. I said, "Let's go and take a look at his room, shall we?"

"Hey," he began, "I don't know," but I said quietly, "Come on. This could be serious," and that swayed him.

We went out into the afternoon heat, which struck like a physical blow after the air-conditioned chill of the reception block. The Sunset Beach had been designed around a Hawaiian theme; I could remember when it had been the Waikiki Royal and, I think, the Honolulu before that. A couple of big transplanted palms, higher than the roofline, leaned over a kidney-shaped pool with a scattering of white metal tables and chairs around its edge; from the more expensive rooms you could walk straight out onto the green carpet, while the rest of them looked down from two sides.

"I assumed his bags were in the car," the clerk said as we stepped through an iron gate to cross the pool enclosure. "But if he didn't actually *have* a car . . ."

"Did he go out yesterday morning?"

"I don't know, I wasn't here. I saw him coming back, though. He was kind of weaving across under the lights, as if he'd been drinking."

"Did you smell drink on him?"

"No sir. I wasn't going to get close enough to find out."

His room was up on the second floor, reached by an outside balcony with a bamboo rail. The curtains were drawn, and there was a *Do Not Disturb* sign hanging on the doorknob. We ignored it.

I wasn't sure what I was going to find; at first it looked as if I was going to find nothing. The room didn't even look occupied, the bed unslept in. It had a deep-pile carpet and a color TV, quite a step up from the Paradise; I thought that perhaps he simply lived as well as he could on whatever money came his way, no saving and no planning, just taking it one day at a time.

45

There were no windows in the bathroom, but an extractor fan started to whirr as I turned on the light. Again everything was clean and untouched-looking but here there was a faint, sour smell of vomit in the air that the fan couldn't quite clear. No marks or stains on the toilet bowl.

From behind me the clerk said, puzzled, "There are no towels here. There should be a full set."

I looked around, and he was right. The little guest soaps were still in their wrappings, but the towel rail was empty. "Maybe he used them," I said.

"For what?"

But I didn't answer. I got down on my hands and knees to take a closer look at the wall behind the toilet. This was plain white plaster, not tile, and as such it wouldn't be easy to wipe clean; and there, sure enough, I found some faint red-brown splashes. Blood splashes, I'd have bet on it. They were so slight that you'd have to be looking in order even to notice them.

The tall skinny clerk was watching me, curious. Getting back to my feet, I said, "Listen to me. I'm going to be waiting around here until he gets back. I don't want anybody else to know about this, and I want you to keep out of his way. You're nervous, and it's going to show."

"You're absolutely right I'm nervous. What did he do?"

"Credit card fraud," I said, and saw him relax as surely as if someone had let some of the air out of him. Credit card fraud's a commonplace in the motel business, and suddenly wouldn't seem like any big mystery.

"So that's why he paid cash?" the clerk said. "Because he knew you were after him?"

"That," I conceded, "and a few other things."

He went back to his work, and I went down to the pool. There were plenty of tropical-style bushes around, but this wasn't amateur night; instead of skulking and drawing attention to myself, I picked out a lounger and angled it so that I'd be able to keep an eye on the target room without having to turn my head. Then, with a can of Doctor Pepper from the dispenser under the arch and a magazine that someone else had left lying around earlier, I stretched out like any resident with an afternoon on his hands and nowhere in particular to go.

I was there for quite a while. I may even have dozed off at one point, because suddenly the sky was darkening and the pool area was floodlit and there was somebody in the water swimming circuits with strong, even strokes. It was some blond guy with a deep tan. Not the one I was looking for.

He came by about fifteen minutes later.

I heard the iron gate behind me, but I didn't turn. Moments later he was walking past, not ten feet away – closer than I'd have liked, but it gave me the chance for a good look at his back. The four hundred dollar jacket made me certain that this was him, even without having seen his face; it was right for the description, and wrong for someone so much in need of a haircut.

He went under the arch, and didn't reappear for a while. Two girls came out to join the blond guy, bringing with them a big radio which they set down by the poolside. They didn't get in, just sat and splashed their feet in the water. After a couple of minutes, I saw movement on the stairway up to the balcony; he was ascending now, and I realised what he'd been doing when I saw the flash of white under his arm as he turned to enter his room. He'd been into the laundry to get his towels from the washing machine. Must have been quite a job, getting the blood out of them.

I didn't want to be here when he came back, because I was sure that he'd know me. I left the court and went across the street to where I could lean on someone else's car and pretend that it was mine and that I was waiting for somebody. He came out after about ten minutes, and didn't even look my way. The guy whose car I was leaning on had left his door open and his keys in the ignition, so before I left it I took them out and hid them under his seat. Do people think we've got nothing better to do than to look for stolen vehicles?

I stayed with him, but well back. Now that I knew where he was basing himself, it would be better to lose him than to risk being recognised. He was taking his time; sometimes he'd stop before crossing the street, even if the light said *walk* and there was no traffic around, and he'd kind of sniff the air as if he could read the currents in it. He reminded me of some kind of animal. It made my flesh go all crawly.

We were on Van Buren now, and he seemed to be looking at bars. He'd weigh one up, maybe take a look inside, and then walk on. It was still early, so there wasn't likely to be much business around; but when he came to a place that I knew to be a gay bar, he went inside and didn't come out again.

It was while I was waiting, as the evening traffic became more heavy and the sound of one of our sirens cut through the rumble from three or four blocks away, that a hooker propositioned me. It was that kind of area, and I'd probably taken up a position on her turf which made it a reasonable enough mistake. I looked at her; she was an undernourished-looking black girl in a skimpy blue dress that looked as if it had been made out of somebody's sleeve. Her body was about as appealing as a bag of razor blades, but she had a nice smile. I thought of Loretta, a thought that came so sharply that it almost hurt; and I said thanks for the offer, but tonight I've got other plans, at which she glanced across at the gay bar and rolled her eyes heavenward before she walked away. If she wanted to consider me a lost cause, then that was fine. Just as long as she left me alone.

He came out of the bar after about half an hour, and he was by himself. I got a really good look at him under the streetlights. His face was no longer slack and indifferent, the empty vessel that I'd already seen, but it still looked wrong somehow; after being as good as dead for so long, life seemed to be out of place there. He set off briskly, and with a sense of purpose this time; when he turned the corner and headed north, I had to run across the traffic against a light to keep up.

My guess was that he'd been directed along to another place, having failed to find the action that he was looking for. Whatever that action might be. I tracked him to a small club, another gay venue where a neon sign in the solitary window said CERVEZA BUD and a handwritten notice below that said *Under New Management: No Chains, Studs or Leathers*. I remembered the club from the old days, when some of the boys had concocted a bogus call to send a motorcycle rookie in there to speak to the bartender. The mythology was that half the clientele had fainted on the spot as the rookie strode in wearing the complete Erik Estrada rig.

I couldn't go in after him. He might see me, or somebody might know me. But I was starting to get an idea of what all this might be about, and so I found a doorway and settled down to wait. I was half-tempted to go back and get my car, but I didn't want to chance missing anything.

As it happened I'd have had plenty of time, because he was inside for more than an hour. The evening was starting to move and I counted about fifty people, all male, going in before he finally emerged; and then, when he came out, he was no longer alone.

His companion was short, hardly standing taller than his shoulder, and he didn't look happy. I'd have placed him around my own age, but he was someone who worked to stay young; he wore a checked shirt, tight designer jeans, and his thinning hair was in a close, almost military crop. The corpse put an arm around his shoulder and was talking to him from the door onwards, speaking quietly and earnestly and obviously working hard to persuade; but whatever he was saying it wasn't having any effect, because the short guy was already trying to pull away. I moved out of my doorway and set out unnoticed to cross the street ahead of them, and as I squeezed by a panel truck to make the sidewalk I heard sharp words and something that was almost, but not quite, a scuffle. When they were back in my line of sight, the short guy was already disappearing back into the club and the corpse was alone again.

He seemed unfazed. He started towards me, not seeing me yet because I was in shadow. He was looking at the ground, thinking.

I said, "You're looking lonely."

That stopped him. He probably couldn't see much more of me than a sketchy shape in the darkness, but he picked up the lead quickly; he said, "A lonely guy can always use a friend."

"Got a car?" I said, thinking that if a Vice team were suddenly to appear out of the darkness around us, my whole life and career would instantly have the value of four drops of dog piss on a rainy road.

"I got better than a car," he said smoothly. "I've got a motel room less than two blocks away."

Jeez, what a conman. It was five blocks at least. I said, "Okay, I'll drive us over."

"Can't we walk?"

"Walk?" I said. "Are you kidding me?"

I couldn't get used to hearing his voice. It was like hearing a dead man speak. What made it so strange was that he sounded normal, just like everybody else. All that I wanted to do right now was to get him off the street somehow so that I could prise the story behind the Paradise mystery out of him. I didn't plan to let him slip through my hands like Mercado had.

I led the way around the back of the club, through an open gate in a chain link fence which gave into a yard full of rusting old refrigerators stacked three-deep. A single spotlight shone down from a corner pole, throwing long shadows onto the cinderblock wall that was the back of the club building. Aluminium vents turned on the roof, echoing tinnily with a ghost of the Tina Turner music that was playing inside.

I heard him stop behind me.

"Where is it?" he said.

I was starting to turn, but he was faster. I saw something drop in front of my eyes and reached up in a reflexive gesture to brush it away, and that was what saved me; my fingers were hooked under the noose as he jerked it tight around my neck and my knuckles crushed hard against my throat. He pulled on it again, probably hoping to black me out anyway. It wasn't as thin as piano wire, but it was fine enough to bite into my palm and cause as much concentrated pain as anything I can remember.

I slammed back with my free elbow, but he was expecting this and he caught it; what he *wasn't* expecting was for me to use his own grip to jerk him forward while I stuck my leg in the way. He went sprawling and hit the garbage-strewn ground like a sack, and when he turned over it was to find that he was facing the empty black eye of my Colt. The noose drew off easily without his weight on the other end of it, and I threw it to one side.

50

He stared right past the gun, as if it didn't worry him. He was looking at me.

He said, "You're the cop."

"Yeah," I said, stretching the fingers on my other hand. It felt as if it would glow in the dark. "Now explain to me how you can recognise me."

"I told you," he said. "I don't like questions."

"*You* told me?"

His face went blank for a moment, as if he realised too late that he'd made a serious slip; but then he smiled, and shrugged it off. He made as if to rise from the floor, but I kicked his hand from under him. Nothing fierce, just enough to drop him back.

I said, "Tell me something. How can you live with what you did to that child?"

I hadn't known what response this would provoke. What I got was the return of the smile, spreading wider this time.

I said, "I know it's not feeding. Because you throw up what you eat."

The smile died at that. "You think you know so much," he said, and I recognised the tone of someone who believed himself to be ultimately untouchable.

"I know there's some kind of trick going on here," I said, "and you're going to tell me what it is."

"Even if I did," he said, "you could never prove anything."

And less than one second later he was gone, leaving me with a look of mocking triumph that was frozen onto the face of a once-more empty corpse.

8

At first I stood there dumbly, unable to believe what I'd just seen for the second time. It was as rapid and as total as if someone had simply pulled a plug. Even though I kept the gun on him as I crouched and felt for a pulse, I knew that there was no way that he could be shamming.

I put the gun away. It wasn't my standard Smith & Wesson but a little Colt Detective Special that I'd picked up for cash a couple of years before and which, as far as I knew, couldn't be traced to me. I'd given it a load of half-charged cartridges which didn't make much more of a kick than a distant backfire, because while I hadn't actually set out with anything illegal in mind I'd been wary of getting myself into some kind of corner that I might not be able to explain my way out of.

And here I was.

I hauled the body across the yard and got it up into one of the club's two big garbage hoppers; they were the big, industrial-sized drums that hook onto the back of a collecting truck and get emptied automatically. With any luck he'd be minced and mashed and compacted and finally recycled as the dashboard of a Ford Fairmont, and nobody would ever know. I didn't even think about reporting this. I'd already heard how some of it would sound when I said it out loud.

There was a thump when he hit the bottom of the drum, which was almost empty. I walked out of the alley without looking back and I kept my pace down to the same speed until I was a block away, at which point I started to run. I reached my car about five minutes later, breathless and panting, and then it took me another five to speed up to Roosevelt and the County General with an eye on the mirror for my own people.

I almost didn't make it. I parked with some GSA motor pool cars to get as close as possible to the six-story patient tower, but I couldn't be sure which would be the best exit to cover. I *did* know that they tried to keep the hospital fairly tightly sealed so that the public couldn't simply wander in and out unchecked, but there still had to be service doors and staff exits. I walked along the side towards Emergency Receiving, and suddenly there he was.

He must have known that I was coming, because he was still in his hospital whites with nothing more than an overcoat hastily thrown over. He came running down the wheelchair slope and out into the night, and as soon as he was through the flap doors I was starting after him. He must have seen me because he veered away towards the traffic out on Roosevelt, but I was faster because he was barefoot and I wasn't. If they'd left his soiled old tennis shoes by his bed it might have been a different story, but this way I hit him about halfway across the lot and brought him down. The fall with my weight on top of it drove all the air out of him, but still he tried to struggle from under. I had one of his arms clamped and reached for the other in an attempt to get him cuffed, but he wriggled and fought and so I slammed my fist down between his shoulders with a blow that would have shaken a mahogany table.

He knew that he was cornered. He knew that he was the last of the four from the Paradise, and that there was nowhere else to run. But he was also the strongest and the fittest of all of them, the same kind of build as Mercado only bigger, and he was determined not to stay down. I felt his free elbow come up like a piston into my ribs, and that bought him enough freedom to throw me off and to roll over; but even through the haze of pain I was still hanging onto his wrist, and as he tried to rise I was able to drag him down and hit him around the side of the head on the way. That *really* slowed him, and I got onto his chest and pinned him to the ground as I reached around for the waistband holster in the small of my back where the Detective Special was hidden under my shirt.

He was grinning at me.

"I've seen through the trick," I shouted down at him although there were only inches between us. "I know what you do. You've got all these different faces but you're the same guy every time." And the grin became a laugh, and I said, "Am I right?" And then he was laughing so hard that he was bouncing me up and down and I stopped fumbling for the gun and socked him as hard as I could. His head snapped over to one side but he kept on laughing as if the pain was something that he didn't really feel, and I leaned forward and screamed again, "*Am I right?*" into his ear. I was reaching for the gun again as I did it, as certain as I'd ever been of anything that I had to kill him now as he lay here in the last of his shell-bodies, and that if I could only do this one simple thing there would be no more slack corpses ticking over on fresh air and baby food and no more children bleeding to death with pieces of their bodies torn away.

Two hands clamped around my upper arm then, and someone else caught me from the other side. I was suddenly weightless, heaved up to my feet with the blind fury draining out of me as I stood.

"You don't beat up on the patients," one of the orderlies holding me said. "That's what they pay *us* for."

9

The Chief looked me in the eye and said, "Explanations, Alex?"

"I mistook the man, sir."

"You don't say?"

It was now the next morning, and I was on the carpet in the Chief's office. The Chief was behind his big desk and Lieutenant Michaels was sitting to one side, looking uncomfortable and meeting nobody's eyes. I could almost feel sorry for him; he was the man in the middle with no firm place to stand, while my position at least was absolutely indisputable. I was firmly in the ordure.

I also had the sense of being an exhibit as I stood there to attention with my uniform cap under my arm, because although the Chief's office was fully enclosed and sound-proofed its walls were two-thirds glass that looked out into the rest of the department; and the rest of the department, of course, looked in. The whole design was supposed to promote a sense of accessibility, but all that it promoted in me was a feeling of being a small bug on a large white piece of paper. I doubted that there was anybody in the building who didn't by now know what I was here for; and I was certain that there was nobody who'd listen to the true story and believe it.

So I said, "I was driving by. I saw him coming out at a run with a couple of people on his tail, it seemed reasonable to slow him down a little so that I could find out what was going on."

"Slow him down a little? From the way the ward orderlies tell it, you were trying to reshape his face."

"Heat of the moment, sir. All I did was give him a little tap when he started to fight me."

The Chief sat back, looking at the single sheet of memo paper on his otherwise empty desk; empty, that is, apart from the telephone and the blotter and a family photo and a couple of paperweight-sized bronze trophies whose inscriptions I wasn't close enough to read. The Chief was young for his office, dark and good-looking and with a knack of being able to remember everybody's name without having to grope for it like the rest of us have to. I'd had him classed as a born politician from the first time that I'd seen him.

Looking up from the paper, he said, "You weren't in uniform."

Lieutenant Michaels said, "Sergeant Volchak was off-duty yesterday."

"Like I said," I insisted, "I was only passing. First thing that had come into my mind was that we had a junkie tried to make a snatch from the Emergency Room. It's happened before."

"Whatever the justification," the Chief said, "the fact remains that we're on very shaky ground here if we get a complaint. You know I've got to suspend you."

"I understand that, sir."

Turning to the Lieutenant, he said, "What's the situation, Dave? Do we have a complaint here, or what?"

Michaels checked his own notes. Somebody walked by outside, and I resisted the impulse to turn to see who it was.

He said, "Nothing's been submitted yet, but I think we've got to assume that it's going to happen. Mr . . ." He searched for a name. "Mr Woods is news this morning. He was one of the three men found in the Paradise Motel and misdiagnosed as brain-dead."

He raised his eyes from his notes to look at me then, I think for the first time.

He added, "Sergeant Volchak took that call."

They were both staring at me, now. The Chief said, "Jesus, Alex," and I could only shrug, uncomfortably.

Mister Woods, I was thinking, and I was wondering if he'd picked the name at random or whether it had any significance from his past. God, how I was bursting to tell them what had really happened, but I could imagine their faces if I did. Somehow I couldn't see the light of understanding dawning as I explained that the one they were calling Woods now carried the memories and the responsibilities of the Encanto Park torture-killer. The best I could hope for would be a nice new canvas jacket with a lot of straps and buckles down the back. Woods, meanwhile, would be walking around on the outside.

It was the worst interview I'd ever had, but it came to an early end because the Chief had to attend a press conference to report the progress of the investigation over that same Encanto Park business. The word within the service was that the investigation was getting nowhere, with no leads, no evidence, no witnesses, nothing. A search of the records had brought up a number of similar cases in the past, both in Phoenix and in other states and cities, but there was nothing that could be related.

Of course not, I thought.

I got the feeling that the Chief was relieved that my story at least held together, and that as long as it continued to hold together he wasn't about to start poking and testing and trying to make holes. But when he'd gone and I was about to follow him out, Lieutenant Michaels closed the door after him and stood in the way.

He said, "You got anything else to tell me, Alex?"

"There's no connection, Dave," I lied. "How could there be?"

"That's what I've been trying to work out. You've never seen Woods outside of these two occasions?"

"Never." In one sense, this much was true.

"I just don't get it."

"It was a straight mistake."

"You can bullshit the top man, Alex, but don't try it with me, all right? You weren't passing, you were in the parking lot. You were already out of your car. You were on top of a

56

guy who just crawled out of a hospital bed and it took two fit men to haul you off. They're saying you were really trying to do the guy harm."

I was lucky that they hadn't made it to me five seconds later, by which time I'd have had the gun out from under my shirt; ten seconds, and maybe Woods would have been history. He'd been at the end of the line, with no more bodies prepared and waiting. But now that he was free and walking, I'd no doubt that he'd already have begun to set that situation right.

Michaels said, "The Chief wants you to see a doctor."

"A shrink?" I said.

"Will you consider for a minute that he might be right? You've been getting too close to the job. You've got no home life, no social life, and now this. I'm going to make the appointment, and you're going to keep it."

"Is that an order?"

"You're damn right it is."

He opened the door to walk out ahead of me, and as he turned away I said, "What's the story from the hospital?"

He stopped, and wouldn't give me a straight look. "They're firing a few junior people and saying it's what they always suspected," he said grudgingly, and then he went out.

My suspension was effective immediately, so I had nothing to do other than to drive over to the Sky Harbor station, change out of my uniform, and then go home. I'd already handed over my badge; my service revolver was my own. I've no doubt that I was wrong, but I couldn't shake the feeling as I waited for the elevator to take me down to the ground floor that the sole topic of conversation in the offices and corridors around me was Alex Volchak's unprofessional outburst. It was ridiculous, this wasn't even my building. Most people here didn't know my name.

So now I was supposed to see a shrink. I wouldn't argue, but I also wouldn't go. I had other things to do.

When I stepped out of the elevator, Woods was there.

He was over at the enquiry counter next to the recruitment desk, half turned-away from me but instantly recognisable. He was wearing creased-looking off-white pants and a new shirt with some kind of tropical fruit or flower design all over it. He was leaning forward on the counter, his brawny arms taking his weight, as the desk sergeant laid out forms before him and explained what I assumed would be the complaints procedure in detail. At that same moment three plain clothes people, two young men and a girl, were knocking on an office door by the elevators and one of them called out, "Come on, or I'll kick it down," before the door opened and they all walked in laughing. The desk sergeant glanced up from the forms at this, saw and recognised me, and tried wordlessly to point me back towards the holding cell corridor and the rear exit; but Woods had seen him and was already beginning to turn around, and I walked straight over.

It was there as soon as our eyes met; we shared a knowledge that was unique. Woods was leaning on one elbow, smiling pleasantly out of a face that I wouldn't have trusted to tell me the time.

He said to the desk man, "That's all right, I'm not going to make a scene. I understand that there's nothing personal in this. Isn't that right, Sergeant Volchak?"

"It's okay, Joe," I told the desk man. He didn't look happy, but he did look relieved and a little puzzled.

Woods said, "You mistook me for somebody else, right? It happens."

"I've heard that it can," I said. My voice in my own ears sounded flat and neutral, which was the way that I wanted it to be.

Woods gathered up his forms, and made a *shall we?* gesture towards the main doors. As I went ahead of him out onto the sidewalk, I saw him drop the papers into a waste basket before following me.

"You're not making a complaint?" I said, as we moved aside to let a visitor party through.

"Too much trouble," he said, and I knew then that he'd been waiting for me and that the forms had only been an excuse to hang around. He went on, "If I want to punish you, I can always find a way."

"You've got a good case," I said. "You could get rich."

We stopped, just outside the doors but in nobody's way. He said, "You know I can't use money. Not that kind of money. When I want to move on, it won't travel."

58

Small talk. Who'd have believed it?

I said, "You know you're insane."

He smiled, slowly. "That wouldn't explain it," he said. "*You* being insane, that would be something else. Why can't you just accept what you see?"

I said, "I was supposed to end up like the others, wasn't I?"

"And how would that be?"

"Brain-dead and living on baby food. But for what?"

"Until I came to need another."

This was like pulling teeth. "Another what?"

"Another body, of course." He tapped the side of his head. "In here, this is me. The rest of it, that's just temporary accommodation. I can wear it or I can throw it away for something else."

"Can you prove that?"

"You've seen me do it twice, what more proof do you need? Get with it, Alex."

I said, "You're enjoying this."

"Of course I am," he said. "I almost never get to talk about my work."

I studied him in the sunlight, wondering how much of what I was seeing was on the outside and how much came from within. This incarnation – there didn't seem to be any better way of thinking about it – came over as perhaps a dishwasher who worked out with weights in his bedroom to impress the kind of woman who'd never give him a second glance. He could smile and be calling you his pal in one minute, and then be breaking your arm in the next. And he'd probably still be smiling, even then.

I said, "What *are* you?" And I saw his face turn serious.

"I don't know," he said. "I've been around so long, even I don't remember." And then he said, "You can't touch me, Alex. Think about it. You can never pin me down."

"Don't bet on it."

"I already have. Draw your gun. Blow me away. And then try explaining what you did to your people in there."

He was already ahead of me. I'd been thinking what would happen if I simply took him now. I could pull my .38 and as good as blow his heart out right there outside the headquarters door, watch him fly backwards and fall to lie drumming his heels on the sidewalk until his nervous system finally got the message and gave in. But we both knew that it wasn't going to happen; he'd already had a night and most of a morning to set up his 'insurance', to finish the work that I'd interrupted the previous evening, and I'd simply be wasting my time. Something would fly across the city – I saw it in my mind as something like an invisible bird – and somewhere in another rented room the eyes of a former citizen would open ready for new business.

"Killing the body's the quickest way to do it," he said. "You've seen me manage without but I'll be honest with you, Alex, it's a bind."

Even without that certainty, I doubt that I'd have had the nerve. Not there, not in the knowledge that my own life would be as good as over from that moment. Looking at what he was and what he'd done, perhaps it might have seemed worth the sacrifice; but I'd never thought of myself as any kind of a saint, and I simply wasn't up to it.

"Why tell me?" I said.

"I'm telling you nothing you don't already know," he said pleasantly, but there was a streak of something way back that might even have been pain. "And it gets me out of the darkness for a time. Maybe I just need to be appreciated once in a while."

I said, "At least, go somewhere else," and immediately I could see that I'd reached him and rubbed somewhere sore. His smile died, and something harder and uglier showed through.

"Don't give me orders," he said sharply. "I do what I want."

One moment later, and his irritating confidence had returned. He said, "Well, I'll see you around," and then he turned and walked away from me in the direction of the civic plaza. He might be news this morning, but he obviously wasn't *big* news; I saw one of the radio reporters from KTAR, her recorder slung around her shoulder like a shoeshine box, pass by him without a second glance as she hurried in for the Chief's conference.

There was no point in my trying to follow, not now that he knew me so well. He could as good as disappear, simply dump the body and fly, any time that he wanted to. He was so cocky about it, he didn't even look back.

An invisible bird.

A phoenix, maybe.

10

After a call at Sky Harbor Station to get into civilian dress – which, since I now had nowhere formal to go, consisted of jeans and one of my old Marine Corps shirts – I headed all the way down Seventh Avenue to the South Mountains and the Rod & Gun Club's firing range. It was a long, dry and dusty drive, and I saw little traffic apart from a couple of pickup trucks that came swimming up out of the heat haze, one after another, at one place where the road dipped. When I got there I had the range to myself, and I spent half an hour putting more than three dozen rounds through the Detective Special to work on my aim and to work off some of my anger. But somehow it didn't help – for every paper target that I destroyed, another one came up fresh and clean in its place.

I'd been uncomfortable in the short time that I'd spent in the station. I'd felt a little like a plague carrier; everybody had a word of sympathy or understanding, behind which they were holding back and hoping that the taint of irrational behavior wouldn't spread. After the range, with my wrist sore and my ears ringing in spite of the mufflers, I set out for home. It was now about an hour since I'd parted from Woods on the headquarters steps.

The first thing that I saw when I got in through the door was a folded note that had been pushed through and which was caught between the door itself and the inner mesh screen. I picked it up and opened it out, and saw the words *IRA terrorists* as I recognised Mrs Moynahan's careful and eccentric handwriting. The IRA terrorists, as far as I'd been able to understand, were a team of Mormons who'd been visiting door-to-door a month ago. I filed the note in my Moynahan Dossier – aka the trash – and switched on the radio to catch the lunchtime news and the Chief's conference.

The coverage was by the girl from KTAR. I'd seen her at crime scenes a few times; she had sexy green eyes and a good reporting style, and I'd never been able to understand why she hadn't been snapped up for television until Loretta had pointed out to me that TV news organisations preferred their women to be either bimbos or ballbreakers, with no allowance for the reasonable middle ground between. What emerged from the conference was an official theory that the killer had packed his bags and run, end of story. I thought that it was a little early to expect the media people to swallow that one, and apparently so did they; the Chief got a hard time out of it, but came through as if he'd been greased.

Unlike the Chief I *knew* that he was to do it again, either as Woods or as somebody else. Even though I believed that the mutilation took place to satisfy a perverted want rather than an actual need – hence the throwing-up afterwards – I was sure of a repeat performance because I'd made the mistake of asking him to move on. *Nobody tells me what to do*, he'd said; and now he was going to prove it.

I heard Georgie getting home then, and I leaned back in my chair so that I could look out of the window without being seen; she was alone, opening the door with a key that was on the end of a long piece of string attached somewhere about her person. When she'd disappeared inside the door banged to a couple of times, and I saw her briefly pass the window opposite on her way towards the kitchen. I knew that she'd only walked from the bus to the house, a matter of fifty yards or so, but still the thought of her alone and unprotected made me go cold. I wondered about suggesting to Loretta that she should take a few more days off and we'd go up to Sedona or somewhere, all three of us leaving the city with its prowling beast so that some other mother's child could be taken. But even as I thought of it, I knew that it was a sneaky way out which would solve nothing; and sooner or later we'd have to come back, and when we came back he could still be waiting.

That was when I heard Loretta's jeep, and I quickly got to my feet. I saw her bounce out of the Renegade and up the wooden steps into her own house; I got a vague echo of her calling through to check on Georgie, and of Georgie's reply, and then Loretta was out again and crossing over towards my porch.

She came in. She was flushed and all lit up, like someone slightly intoxicated by a taste of success.

I said, "How'd you get on?"

"I saw you talking to him on the steps," she said as she went over towards my table. I followed her, and pulled out the chair opposite. "I'm glad you did that, or I wouldn't ever have recognised him. The picture you showed me didn't even come close."

"That's thanks to Lightnin' Leslie. He couldn't draw a crowd if his dingus was on fire. Were you spotted?"

"No way. Want a rundown on the details?"

"I'm all ears."

We sat head-to-head across the baize, and Loretta took out one of those small jotting pads that fold into a little pocket-sized wallet. I'd never thought of them as being useful for much other than shopping lists or very short memory-joggers, but I could see that she'd fitted about a dozen numbered points in tiny writing on the first page. She held it squarely before her in both hands. She was enjoying this.

"When he left you," she said, "he went down to the corner and stood there for two, three minutes. He was just watching the traffic, like he couldn't quite decide which way he wanted to go."

I thought of him the previous evening when he'd walked out in another form, stopping at an intersection and scenting the night as if he could read all of its patterns in the air. I said, "When did you make the notes?"

"Afterwards, while it was all still fresh. Don't worry, Alex, I didn't give myself away. After he'd been standing around for a while he walked east a couple of blocks and bought a newspaper. He took it into a coffee shop and sat reading about himself for twenty minutes. Every now and again he'd take a really good, hard look out of the window. I think he was watching for you."

"Did you go into the shop?"

"I didn't want to get that close. I pretended I was waiting at the bus stop across the street."

"Neat."

"Yeah, but wait until you hear the next part. I look over and he's coming out of the shop and heading straight over towards me. I thought he was going to say something, but he'd seen that the bus was on its way and he was more interested in that."

"Did he get on?"

"He did, but I didn't. I kind of checked my watch and made like I wanted some other destination. I didn't want to be on there with him and then have to get off at some stop miles from anywhere. He'd know I was following him if *that* happened. So what I did was, I ran back to where I'd left the jeep and then I picked up the bus again about a mile and a half down the road. He stayed on until right out into Tempe. I think he was just staring out of the window until he saw the kind of place he was looking for, because he got off and went straight across into this dingy-looking hotel. I got a note of the name and address, just like you wanted."

She slid one of the detached pages across to me. No rings these days, I noticed. The hotel name wasn't one that I recognised; but then, Tempe's outside of my area.

I said, "You did well. Pick a prize."

"I'm not finished yet," she said, and out came a second slip. "Here's his room number."

"How did you get that?"

"I went in and charmed the desk clerk."

I felt then like somebody must feel who walks into a strange graveyard and sees his own name on a headstone. This was exactly what I hadn't wanted to happen, and I'd tried to tell Loretta so without actually having to explain to her why I needed to know where Woods was going to base himself next. Apart from the immediate physical danger that I'd barely been able to hint at, there was the chance that he'd take a scare and move on again after only a few hours. The secret of his survival lay in his ability to break a trail with total success; this slim continuity was my only chance of keeping a track of him.

I said, "I wish you hadn't done that."

"There's no harm, Alex," Loretta insisted. "I was careful."

How could I tell her that careful wasn't enough? I said, "He'd already seen you at the bus stop. What if he saw you again?"

"He didn't."

"He might have seen you from the window of his room, and you wouldn't even know it. Or else the clerk could say that someone's been asking after him and the whole thing's blown."

"Now, come on, Alex," she said, closing the notebook with ominous firmness and laying it flat with her hand on top of it, "you asked me for help, and I did you a damn good job."

I had, and she had, and if there was any blame around in this then it was mine and mine alone. "I know, I'm grateful," I began, but she was already on her feet.

"Well," she said, "you could try showing it," and then she stormed out.

11

Perhaps I should never even have asked her. It was easy to think that way now. Or perhaps I should have told her more – but how could I have told her more without telling it all? The fact was that there had been nobody else that I could have relied on, and so I'd put her into danger – the one decent thing that had come into my life of late that hadn't been tied to my work, and I still hadn't been able to keep her out of it. Just sitting and trying to see a way around the problem gave me dull pain behind the eyes. After a while, I heard her go out again. I couldn't deny that she'd gone to a lot of trouble for me. I knew that she'd taken a lot of sanctimonious tut-tutting from her jumped-up junior supervisor to get the couple of hours that I'd asked her for.

And the information that she'd brought me was gold-dust. I had a line on Woods and – hopefully – Woods wasn't aware of it. And something else I now knew; when we'd been standing there and talking out on the street he'd still been alone, no refuge set up and nowhere to fly to, and only afterwards had he begun the process of finding a new lair.

I could have ended it. If only I'd known it then, and had the nerve.

I didn't go out for the rest of the afternoon, or that evening. I hung around the house watching the rooms go dark and trying to straighten out the details, knowing all the time that somewhere out in Tempe there would be somebody suffering something that would be worse than dying, becoming an empty shell to provide the new face of the beast.

I slept badly that night, and dreamed the usual dream of Eloise, only this time it was with a new and unpleasant variation. When she looked up at me, the eyes weren't hers; nothing else in the dream changed, and I was walking her out of the hospital trembling with the need to tell somebody, but everyone we passed simply smiled because the two of us always looked so good together.

The mail came early, when I was showered and dressed and taking the canvas weapon roll out from under my bed. I got one letter, a single sheet of classy headed notepaper in an off-white envelope, and it was from a Doctor Elaine Mulholland inviting me along to an appointment three days hence at her downtown office. Elaine Mulholland, I gathered, was the department-appointed shrink, although there was nothing on the headed paper to suggest as much. I dropped the letter in the Moynahan File on my way out with the roll under my arm.

For all the time that I'd lived in the city, I didn't know Tempe too well; I suppose I tended to think of it as the suburb around the State University and little more than that, when I thought of it at all. They had their own police, and although the adjacent forces shared manpower when necessary I'd never done much more than pass through. I drove east out of Phoenix on Washington, crossing a high concrete bridge over a riverbed that was nothing more than dry gravel. This was the Salt River, which gave its name to an Indian reservation beginning just a couple of miles to the north-east. *Welcome to Tempe*, a sign to my left said as it flashed the time and temperature, *Home of the State University and the Fiesta Bowl*. It was still early, and it was cool. The sign was backed by the high towers of a flour mill and a rocky hillock on the side of which was a big painted *A* facing the sky.

After a railroad crossing, the speed limit dropped to thirty and the town proper began. I was driving with the air conditioning switched off and my window rolled down, a service habit born of the need to keep an ear cocked for the sounds of the night. What I saw now in bright daylight was a low-rise town in the slow process of bringing itself up-to-date with the modern campus at its heart, watched over by occasional tall palms that soared upwards out of the gray dust alongside the road. Many of the two-story shopfronts were scaffolded and in the process of getting a new concrete facing, and most of them in that first, tight mile seemed to be given over to bookshops and poster stores and pizza restaurants. The road was mostly following the edge of the campus here, but after a while it swung left and began to open out again.

The Tropicana Hotel was one of the places that was obviously going to be left behind if it didn't get a change of ownership, a change of purpose, and a lot of money spent on bringing it up to scratch. While it wasn't exactly a flophouse, for many it would be a stage on the way down towards one; pink-stuccoed and peeling, it stood three stories high and held the remnants of its old dignity around it like a falling towel. I cruised past, seeing it as Woods had seen it first from the bus. I had the feeling that I'd have been able to pick it out even if Loretta had lost him somewhere along the way; it was almost as if, after the Paradise and the Sunset Beach, I was getting some kind of feel for his tastes. The hotel faced out across the street onto a huge parking lot, beyond which were tennis courts and, beyond these, tall campus residential blocks.

The juxtaposition gave me a little chill. It was like seeing a hawk set up in a tree overlooking a chicken run. Whatever sat inside Woods, it had shown a taste for young life; and here, young life flowed by like a river. I pulled off the road and looked for a space in the lot.

There was room directly opposite the Tropicana but I didn't want to be so close, not so that I could be seen. When I saw another car leaving and throwing up a high dust, I followed the cloud and took the empty space. The cars around me were Pintos, Volkswagens, some open jeeps like Loretta's; they were mostly compacts or sub-compacts, with the occasional Pontiac or Oldsmobile. One thing that they had in common was that, almost without exception, their paint glazes had been burned matt by the desert sun. Getting out I saw a young blonde girl in yellow shorts and trainers going by, a radio in her shoulder bag tuned low to an FM station, and I wanted to call over to her to go home and lock her door, but I didn't. Instead I went out across the street, and stayed close to the buildings as I walked down towards the Tropicana.

What came next was ridiculously easy. When I entered the small, dim foyer there was nobody behind the desk and no sign of any building security at all, just a wire basket full of cleaning things on the counter and a door open to where a radio was playing loud two or three rooms away. I was able to reach across and lift Woods' key off its hook, and I was away up the stairs before anybody had appeared.

His room was on the fire-escape side of the second floor, and the presence of his key in the foyer indicated that he'd be out. There was the usual *Do Not Disturb* sign hanging on the handle, and I left it in place as I opened up and slipped inside.

My hand was on the Colt Special, just in case, but as I got in and took a look around the room I let it fall the quarter-inch back into its holster. Woods wasn't here although the room, as I'd expected, wasn't empty. The curtains were drawn, and somebody lay on the cheap iron-framed bed.

He was a college kid, as I'd feared. He was tanned and healthy-looking, probably an athlete, and I wondered how Woods had managed to get him to come back here; even if the kid was gay he could almost certainly do better than this, but then Woods probably had a number of different techniques of misdirection and entrapment that he'd have developed over the years. With the fire escape handy, it could all have happened somewhere else; Woods looked strong enough to carry a body upstairs, even a body like this.

I switched on the lights for a closer look.

He was lying with the pillows propped up behind him, so that he wasn't flat; Woods had loosened the boy's belt and laces and had taken off his wristwatch, leaving a pale tan line where the band had been. The watch itself was on the bedside table. He was lying with his hands down by his sides, the fingers slightly curled and his hands turned slightly outward. He looked like a puppet whose strings had been cut. His breathing was shallow, but even.

The ceiling creaked almost directly above me. I stopped and listened, but there was nothing more until a door slammed somewhere deep within the building. I realised that I'd been holding my breath.

I wasn't used to this, creeping around and feeling edgy. I was more used to being the Man with the Badge, the bringer of some kind of order even when that order was sometimes no more than an illusion that disappeared again when the last of the squad cars pulled out. But now my badge was in somebody's desk drawer, and I wasn't even playing on my home turf, and for both I could thank something whose nature and abilities I could barely comprehend.

There was nothing around the college boy's neck, so I carefully unbuttoned his shirt and pulled it open. I was looking for a bruise or some sign of a blow to the chest. There are supposed to be martial arts moves that can deliver a specific localised shock which can stop the heart without causing much more than superficial physical damage, but I saw no evidence of anything like that here. It was when I lifted his chin for a closer look at his throat that I found what I was looking for; the thin, inflamed garotte-line was there all right, but it had disappeared into a crease with the tilt of his head. A minute's further searching turned up a loop of twine similar to the one that had been used on me. It was waxed, and near-impossible to break.

There must have been a certain finesse involved in getting the right tension and holding it for as long as would be needed to starve the brain of blood until the spark of life flickered and died. And then what? Perhaps the new intelligence slipped in for a few moments to restart the heart and the breathing, just check all the dials and the valves and leave everything ticking over on a low maintenance level to await future occupancy.

I didn't have to be so delicate. First I tried rolling him over, the simple technique that had stopped the breathing and then finally finished off one of the three residents of the Paradise, but this boy was strong and healthy and he did little more than rasp and spit into the pillow. As I turned him back, I could hear some of the fluids inside him gurgle.

This was terrible. I felt lower than I'd ever felt in my life before. I took the noose and slipped it over his head and pulled it tight. I'd seen a pencil lying alongside some cheap hotel stationery by the window, and I took this and slipped it under the loop and used it to wind the noose even tighter so that it as good as disappeared into the flesh around his neck, right along the same line as before. The college boy didn't react, or resist. He simply switched off.

I felt sick; but not as sick, I noted, as I perhaps should have felt. I was cold and sweating and my heart was thumping. I'd been in the room for a little over fifteen minutes. I planned to go now, leaving the garotte in place to block any attempt to restart operations.

But before I left I quickly wiped over anywhere that I might have touched, which was how I came to find that my name and address and even my phone number were written in pencil on the hotel paper by the window.

Nobody saw me leaving, either, and I practically ran down the street and over to the car. My plan had been to stick around and wait for Woods to return, somehow to play it by ear; I had every gun that I owned in the trunk of the car, including a hunting rifle with a scope sight accurate enough to take him out as he walked from the bus stop to the Tropicana. I knew that there was at least a chance that I'd come under suspicion for the killing because of my prior assault on him, but I also knew that there wasn't time to mess around. It had to be done now, before he could find out that his escape route had been cut off.

I was here, looking for him; and he was at my place, looking for me. I had to keep the advantage, break the symmetry.

Barely more than five minutes after leaving the hotel, I was recrossing the Salt River into Phoenix.

As I drove, some of my doubts from the previous evening began to rise again. Not doubts about what I was doing – that was clear-cut enough for me, based on the certainties of what I'd seen and what had been said – but about my chances of success. Most of what I knew about this thing that I was fighting came from speculation and deduction; it wasn't like in the books, where someone pops up halfway along with all the answers discovered in some ancient manuscript and then it's an all-action race to the finish. If, for example, it turned out that this parasite could simply hang around in the ether if there was no host on offer, cruising the morgues and the intensive care units on the lookout for something suitable, then I'd be, to put it mildly, in deep shit.

I stopped the car a block south of the residential site and went in over the wall at a point where I knew the Elroys' orange trees would give me cover. I had the Special drawn and in my mind I was nineteen years old again and stalking that weird ghost town with its cardboard pop-up assassins in every doorway and window and live ammo to off them with. I'd made the third highest score in my unit; even the top-scorer had managed to snuff at least one cardboard civilian, but hey, this was war. I forget the name of the town. It was some mining place, but nobody had lived there in years.

I was hopping the picket fences from one garden plot to another, using the houses themselves to screen me as I worked my way around to get an angle on my own place. I had one big advantage in that most of the people on the site were either half-blind or half-deaf or both; the houses were close together and the gardens were dense with green bushes and trelliswork, and the only problem was that while I had perfect cover, so did he.

There was my house; a big through lounge with picture-window, two bedrooms, two bathrooms, two years still to pay. It seemed somehow strange from this unusual angle, as if I was looking at an imperfect copy but couldn't place my finger on any difference in detail. Damn it, all the plots were so close together, there were more hiding places than there were in a maze. I crouched low and waited for a minute or so, but nothing seemed to be happening; all that

I could hear was the steady *swish-swish* of a lawn sprinkler, somewhere over on the far side of the administration block.

I started to rise; perhaps I could get closer.

A hand took a firm hold of my arm.

12

I came up a lot faster than I'd intended, and with considerably more noise; and Mrs Moynahan, still holding onto my arm, said, "Sergeant Volchak, I have to speak to you."

She was in her gardening clothes and carrying a watering can in her free hand, and if she'd noticed my gun she showed no sign of it. Perhaps she thought I did this all the time, either as a habit or a recreation. This wasn't her garden plot, but I knew that she did some weeding and watering for some of the tenants who were too infirm to manage their own; cutting was handled by two enterprising kids from offsite who brought their own mower and tended the postage-stamp lawns at a dollar a throw.

I said, "I'm kind of in a hurry, Mrs Moynahan. Can it wait?"

"I don't think so. Didn't you get my note?"

"The IRA terrorists."

"They sent a man around. I think they've found out you're with the police."

Why me? Why *now*? I felt almost as if a big target had been painted on my back ready for the start of the Volchak season. Still scanning what I could see of the avenue – wooden cladding, white picket, the nose of a car sticking out here and there like that of a sleeping dog – I said, "They won't be a problem any more, Mrs Moynahan. I've had all your information put into the computer, they're moving on it right now . . ."

"Please, Sergeant." Her hand was on my arm again, and I had to look at her. It occurred to me that I'd always avoided meeting her eyes before, but now I could see that they were steady and clear. She said, "Please, don't humor me. I know you do, most of the time. But I'm serious."

I could feel myself starting to blush. I suddenly felt as if my house was of glass, and that she knew all about the Moynahan file with its collection of screwed-up notes and tipoffs; there had been times when I'd dug out the latest and smoothed it out to show to some visitor. But now I could sense that there was something very sane shining through the delusion, and I said, "What did he look like?"

"Short and dark, about thirty-five. Strong-looking, like someone who works in the open. He was wearing a flowered shirt and light slacks, not too clean. He tried your door, but he couldn't get in. He was watching around as he did it. He knew he was doing wrong."

"What did he do then?"

"He went to the next house. The young woman's place, I don't know her name. I tried to see what he was doing there, but I couldn't. You didn't believe my note, did you?"

"I believe you now," I said.

Loretta's door was unlocked, but Woods wasn't there. It was worse than that, much worse. When I'd double-checked all the rooms I returned to the lounge, where the TV was playing to nobody and a half-finished TV dinner lay cold on the table.

How long? Half an hour, more? Georgie had been given all of the warnings about strange men and strange cars and strange propositions, but here was somebody whose plausibility had been polished by lifetimes of practice. I didn't doubt that he could conjure up charm when he needed to, although I'd seen nothing of this quality in him so far.

I ran out of the main gates and down to my car.

As long as he was still on foot, I had a chance. The site was in a relatively undeveloped part of the city, in a grid of open desert roads with no more than two or three houses on some blocks and none at all on others; even where the development became heavier along the canal, the area still kept the feel of some dry and dusty suburb of little traffic and a lot of space. I couldn't guess which direction he might have chosen; north towards Indian School Road, perhaps, drawn through the morning's haze by the distant red mountains, or south to the heavy buildup and intermittent sleaze of Van Buren?

I quickly circled the immediate few blocks. I'd lived here for some time, but I knew nobody outside of the site itself. There were no shops and nowhere to socialise, so how could I? As I realised with some alarm after my second wrong turn, I didn't even know the layout of the streets too well. Put me in the Deuce, and I could almost drive around blindfold. Here, I was making big tyre-arcs in the dust and heading back the way I'd come within the first couple of minutes.

There were people around, but not many. Two dried-out looking old women sat on folding chairs that they'd taken from their station wagon and set on the white concrete levee overlooking the canal, facing the sun and baking in the glare as if they hoped it might preserve them for a little while longer; and when I called to them and they turned to me, I saw that they were both wearing little black round-lensed sunglasses like radiation goggles. They hadn't seen anyone. They hadn't seen anything. They didn't want to know.

I covered more ground, getting nowhere. The further out that I drove, the thinner my chances of success became. At one junction I was checking around so desperately that I almost tailgated a pickup truck that had stopped in front of me, but I scorched to a halt with maybe an inch to spare. The owner was getting out and wanted to fight; I showed him the Special and he turned around and slowly walked back to his vehicle and climbed in, moving as if the ground was almost too hot to bear. He followed me at a distance for a block or so, but I managed to lose him.

I asked everybody I saw, which was maybe three people, "Did a man and a girl go by here? A little girl, about so big?" And I raised my hand to approximate Georgie's height. They all shook their heads, none of them spoke out loud.

None except the telephone linesman.

He was sitting in his truck and eating a sandwich as he ran a ballpoint down some list on a clipboard. I had to get out of my car to go and talk to him, but I left the engine running.

Yeah, he'd seen a man and a girl not ten minutes ago. The little girl was holding onto the man's hand and they were walking north on forty-seventh, one block west of the canal.

I thanked him, and almost flew back across the road. Holding his hand? I'd cut his damned hands off, both of them, for even touching her. I gripped the wheel hard and tried to control myself; drive slowly and give no warning, I told myself, as my anger and fear boiled inside like something sour.

Wrong man. Wrong girl.

He was in his sixties and must have weighed about three hundred pounds, while the child – probably his grand-daughter – couldn't have been much more than five years old. He was wearing a red sweater, and the two of them walking along and talking about this and that bore an uncanny resemblance to Winnie-the-Pooh and Piglet. They both looked up as I hit the accelerator and took the bend just ahead of them, and the child pointed and said something.

I was so frantic now that I wasn't thinking straight; because although they weren't the people that I was looking for, it still made sense to ask them what they'd seen.

So when I reached the canal, I began to turn so that I could circle back and speak to them; which was how I hit the jackpot.

Woods and Georgie were about a hundred yards further down, walking with their backs to me. They were over on the other side of the canal, partly screened by the red-earth levee that had replaced the concrete for this section. Woods was talking, but he wasn't touching her. Neither looked back as I completed the turn as quietly as I could; then, as soon as they were out of sight, I put my foot down and raced up the parallel street to get ahead of them. Pooh and Piglet watched me pass for a second time, seeming no less demented now than before.

I left the car on Osborne, and ran the last half-block. The canal made a short dogleg here so that it crossed under-neath the street; they'd have to pass over the bridge, and this would be where I'd wait. The canal was unfenced, a short scramble down the levee to where the water ran black and slow, and I could get down and hug the hard-baked earth and let them come by within a few feet of me. I drew the Special, safety off, and laid it flat on the ground alongside my face. If I had to use it now, I'd plant it on him afterwards; with a clear case of kidnap here, I'd probably get away with it.

They were coming. I heard Georgie saying, "Are you kidding me? I've been up here before. It doesn't go anywhere."

"All I know is what Alex told me," Woods said. He didn't even sound plausible to me, he just sounded greasy and dangerous. "You don't trust Alex?"

"I don't even think you're a cop."

"Sure I am."

"Where's your badge?"

(Twenty feet)

"I'm in plain clothes. Look, you want to see these new police dogs, or what?"

"How old are they?"

(Passing me now)

"Fifteen weeks. They're just puppies, they still haven't had all their shots. That's why we have to keep them so far out."

I came up silently, the baked earth a perfect footing and making no sound; I was so close that I almost betrayed myself with my shadow instead. Georgie was too much in the way for me to fire, but I took one long step and swung the butt of the revolver in an arc over her head. Woods saw it coming and began to turn – his reactions were fast, all right – but I caught him on the temple and spun him around. Georgie shrieked in surprise as he fell, but I had to leave her as I tossed the gun behind me where he wouldn't be able to reach it and then got a grip on his collar. He was making strange grabbing motions at the air with his hands, as if he wanted to hold his head but had lost the co-ordination to find it, and I was easily able to pull him up and get my arm around his throat to shut off his air and everything else with a choke-hold. After only seconds he stopped grasping, and then he slid from my grip and hit the ground ¹ike a sack.

I looked at Georgie. She was watching the whole thing in disbelief, her mouth open and her eyes wide.

Then she said, "I knew he wasn't a cop."

"So why'd you go with him?"

"I was going to run. We're right near Jilly Henderson's. I was going to knock on their door."

It wasn't my job to get angry with her. I said, "You know the number of the place where your mom works?"

She nodded. I knew that Loretta had made her repeat it over and over, in case of emergency. I thought that this probably qualified.

I said, "Okay. I want you to go on to the Hendersons' and use their phone to call your mother. Ask her to get here as fast as she can. Walk out on the job if she has to, it's that important. And then when you've made the call, stay with the Hendersons until she comes to pick you up. That won't be long."

I got her to repeat the street names and the message, and then I sent her on her way at the usual earth-shaking run. Even before she was out of sight I'd retrieved and re-holstered the Special and began to roll Woods over the lip of the levee to where he could lie without being seen from the road.

I was watching him carefully. The butt of the revolver had bruised his temple without breaking the skin, and the choke-hold had left no mark at all. He was twitching and his eyes were moving under their lids, both good signs; they meant that he was genuinely unconscious and hadn't been able to desert the body. When he seemed on the point of coming around, I choked him again. You can do a person serious damage that way, but this was the least of my worries. I had to do it twice more before Loretta got there.

She was in the jeep, as I'd been hoping. I stood up and waved her in as soon as I saw her, and she pulled over to park on the shoulder of the road just below me. Standing up to get out, she said, "Alex? What is all this?"

"I need your help again," I said. I was aware that we hadn't spoken since our stormy scene of yesterday; and so, obviously, was she.

"This had better be good, Alex," she said as she stepped up the embankment towards me. "I don't even know that

I've got a job to go back to." She wasn't able to see the body at my feet until she was almost at the crest; and then, when she could, she did a perfect double-take. She said, "Is that Woods?"

"He came looking for me," I said. "He took Georgie instead. He's the Encanto Park killer. He thinks he can never be caught."

I'd never actually seen the colour drain from anybody's face in an instant before, but Loretta was suddenly so pale with shock that it was almost as if someone had shone a light through her.

"He *took* her?" she managed to say.

"Fed her some story. It wasn't her fault."

She looked down at Woods again. He wasn't exactly a sympathy-inspiring sight at the best of times, and now as far as Loretta was concerned he was less so than ever.

"Kill him, Alex," she said. "Don't take him in. Kill him. Do it now."

"Lend me your jeep," I said.

"Are you going to do it? Because if you won't, I will."

"I'm going to stop him for good. He doesn't think I can, but he's wrong. Can I have the jeep for a couple of hours?"

She nodded, her mind only half-on my request. She was probably remembering the reports on the Encanto Park child murder; details were still coming out, and the TV stations had each come up with a special graphic symbol to flash up behind their anchor people whenever the story featured in a bulletin.

I said, "My car's just around the corner. There are some things I need in the trunk. Can you bring it?"

By the time that she got back with my car, I'd dragged Woods down from the levee and hoisted him up into the jeep's passenger seat. He slumped there, still out of it. Loretta stood well back and watched as I opened up the trunk of my car and transferred the canvas roll across to the open rear of the Renegade; she wasn't quite so pale now, and that sudden certainty had gone.

I said, "Georgie's up at the Henderson house."

"I know."

"Use my car again and take her home. I'll join you sometime later."

She saw me handcuff Woods securely to the overhead roll bar, both hands. He groaned a little. I wanted to get him away from there, before he came around and said something that might make the next stage more difficult.

Loretta said, "What are you going to do?"

"You don't want to know."

"Alex, are you absolutely sure about this?"

"Trust me. He boasted about it to me, that's how safe he thinks he is. And he took Georgie, remember."

That swayed it for her, but I could still see a reluctance in the way that she left. First came the thirst for blood, but afterwards came the doubts. Something I couldn't afford.

I got behind the wheel of the jeep and started the engine. Woods looked like an odd kind of passenger in the cuffs, but they kept him upright and made it look as if he was holding onto the roll bar for safety. At the first major street I turned east, heading for the edge of the city and the desert reservation beyond.

There was a sound from the seat beside me.

13

We were coming up to a simple turnoff, marked by nothing more elaborate than a broken stake with an old car wheel as its base; the sign that it had carried had long gone, and as we turned onto the nameless track I glanced at Woods. He was blinking, and literally didn't know what had hit him. This was what I'd hoped.

I said, helpfully, "It's called a headache."

He turned to look at me, his head moving like something on a stiff bearing. I could almost see the intelligence reassembling itself there, the scattered pieces rapidly coming together in a seamless fit.

"Clever, Alex," he said, and his voice was dry and scratchy. "Very clever. But as a technique, it's annoyance-value only."

"Better than nothing at all," I said.

The road went on into the roughest, poorest country. It was an unmade track, a bare strip of the wide desert plain running all the way out to where the mountains were like heaped stones on the horizon. To either side were cacti, prickly pear, salt bushes; we passed a desert fox which lay bundled at the roadside like an old shirt, days dead.

It wasn't a road that got heavy use, because it led almost nowhere. This was what made it ideal.

Woods said, "Whatever you've got in mind, you're wasting your time."

I glanced at him again. He was looking straight ahead, but that confident and irritatingly superior smile was back. He'd settled into the seat as far as the cuffs would allow, and in spite of his dusty clothes and his bruises and his messed-up hair he had the look of someone who was waiting to be entertained.

I said, "You think so?"

And he said, "Yeah, but don't stop. I can always use a good joke."

"I bet you don't get many, in a life like yours."

I seemed to have hit a nerve with that one, because he didn't reply. He made as if something had caught his interest over to the side, and turned away; I got a brief flash of the dropping of the mask, but I didn't see what was revealed underneath.

"Exactly what are you?" I said. "Really?"

"I'm older than the desert," he said tonelessly. "I don't have a name." When he turned to face front again the facade was back up, but now he was looking more serious. He said, "Don't hate me for what I have to do, Alex."

"What do you expect me to do? Like you for it?"

He shook his head slowly, looking out through the windshield but not focussing on the road ahead. "I don't know why I let you get so close," he said. "No-one else ever has."

Hearing him use my name like he had, it was like having somebody stroke my back with a dead snake; but I wanted to keep him talking and so I said to him, "Answer me one thing. Tell me why you killed the child. And then tell me how many others you've done."

"That's two things."

"Come on, just between us. I know it isn't for food, because you threw up what you ate. Do you get something else out of it? Or is it just some kink?"

He turned to look at me again. He wasn't smiling, his eyes were dead; for one brief moment I was afraid that he'd pulled out and left me with a lifeless shell as a hostage, but then he spoke.

"He was young life," he said.

His voice was remote, like something echoing up from a crack in the earth. Even in the desert heat, I felt the chill wind of the dead blow through me.

"So it's a kink," I said.

His dead eyes seemed infinitely weary. "What do you know about anything?" he said.

"I'm learning all the time."

"Better start counting the time you have left. Because I've got to tell you, Alex, when your little game's finished then so are you. Nothing personal, it's just the cycle. The cycle's all that matters. Predator and prey. It's like a heartbeat, only your kind never hear it. That's the difference between us. That's why I'll always win, and you'll always lose."

"But you *can* die," I persisted.

"Anything can die. But I never will."

There was silence for a while. Our dust trail now went back five miles or more, but the mountains still seemed an infinite distance ahead. We'd seen no life at all, apart from a couple of roadrunners that had dashed across the track in front of the jeep towards the beginning. The sky overhead was the deep, pitiless blue of noon.

Young life. Jesus. Ancient and sour as he was, he must have despised it. He'd worked his way through every pleasure on offer through the ages, and now the only one left to him was to see young life suffer. Revenge on those who had something he'd lost and could never have again.

I slowed the jeep to a halt, but kept the engine running. It was the only sound, out there in the vast bowl of the desert.

"Okay," I said, and I reached up to the roll bar and unlocked the handcuffs. I was wary of him grabbing for me, but he didn't try. He sat rubbing some life back into his wrists, and flexing his fingers.

He said, "What now?"

"You've convinced me. Get out of the car."

"What?"

"Get out of the car. I'm damned if I'm going to drive you back into town."

He was suspicious. Nothing too great, just a tiny grain of disquiet, but I could see that it was nibbling away at the edge of his confidence.

"What are you planning?" he said.

"What does it matter? You're supposed to be untouchable. Now move away from the car."

He got out, stiffly. He stood by the jeep and put his hands into the small of his back and stretched until I could almost hear his joints pop.

I reached over into the back, and came up with the hunting rifle.

"Move," I said, and he started to walk. After a few steps, he stopped and looked back; I could see that he still wasn't entirely certain about this. It wasn't because of the rifle, because that didn't seem to be bothering him at all.

I said, "Something else?"

"The woman and child," he said. "I'll remember them."

But not for long, I thought, and without taking any particular aim I raised the rifle one-handed and fired into the scrub just a yard or so to the side of him. The sound was instantly lost out here in the open, but the rock-dust flew and spattered his legs.

I said, "Keep walking." He was still too close. I didn't want to risk getting anything of him on me, or on the jeep.

He was shaking his head. "Oh, Alex," he said, and I recognised the tone of it; I heard actual affection there, the condescension of a higher species for a lower, an immune observer touched by the frantic but futile efforts of some small beast to do him harm. With a sorrowful smile, he turned and started to walk. He didn't follow the road, but struck out at an angle; as if he'd been here before, and knew where he was, and knew exactly which direction would be the shortest way back.

Perhaps he had. The Salt River Valley had at least a two

82

thousand year history of settlement, but it was a history without details; the Hohokam Indians had faded out and left no writings and very little for the mound-diggers to argue over. They also used to cremate their dead; and I wondered now if I was looking at the reason why.

"Okay," I said, "that's about far enough," and he stopped and turned to face me again.

"You're disappointing me, Alex," he said.

"Answer me one more thing," I said. "Say somebody made it so that you had no more bodies to jump to, and then something happened to you. Say I'd found your boy in the Tropicana and switched off his lights for good. What then?"

He didn't have to reply.

His face had already told me everything that I needed to know.

He turned and he started to run, and I hoisted the rifle up and put my eye to the scope sight. I was standing in the jeep and resting the gun on the roll bar, so my aim was steady. That awful flowered shirt was already beginning to lose its colors with the distance; beyond him, the rising haze from the desert shimmered like meltwater. The crosshairs were almost squarely on the back of his head. He had a balding spot, and I was targeting just below it.

Now look at me, I thought.

It might have been coincidence or it might have been something else, but at exactly that moment I saw him turn to look back over his shoulder and I corrected slightly to re-site the crosshairs. I had the feeling that he was looking straight into my eyes as I squeezed the trigger. I lost the image of him for a moment with the bucking recoil of the gun, but then I found him again and he was still looking back as he ran, only now his head from the eyebrows up was empty space. He took three more staggering steps, like a drunk. Then he folded for good.

I waited, wondering if I was going to hear or feel anything as the bird made one last flight to find its refuge gone. I was tensed-up, but I heard nothing. A faint echo of my shot came back from the mountains, but that was all.

I wondered if he'd seen it coming.

I hoped that he had.

PART TWO

False Dawn

Two days later, we loaded up the Renegade and drove north. In three hours we climbed from the desert plain through the hills and into red rock country, burning in the rays of the mid-morning sun. Georgie was still out of school, Loretta was out of a job, and I still didn't know what was to happen to me as a result of the Woods business; but I'd set up this trip and talked Loretta into it because I needed some time to work on her. I could see what was going through her mind as clearly as if she'd been made of fine glass; she was scared to ask me about what had taken place after I'd driven away and left her by the canal, but she was also troubled by not knowing. It was tearing her up, and she was saying nothing. We must have made a strange pair – Loretta being down and trying not to show it, while I was bursting like a jumping bean with a story that I couldn't tell. What Georgie must have made of us both, I don't know.

The gas jockey at the Mobil station told us that we were lucky, because it was warm for October; Oak Ridge had usually had its first snows by now. I turned to Georgie in the back and said that she'd probably make it to Slide Rock, a kind of natural Wet 'n' Wild ride along a smoothed-out streambed, after all if the weather held. Georgie looked thunderstruck and said that she hadn't packed any swimming stuff, and I said that was okay, in that case she'd have to go all the way along Slide Rock *naked*. And then Georgie fumbled around in the back, and came up with the paper bag that had contained most of our breakfast, and promptly put it over her head.

Loretta smiled a tight little smile, and then told her to take it off.

We drove into Sedona and parked on the wide main street, just across from where the pink-painted tour jeeps were lining up ready for the first excursion of the afternoon. Sedona was still a small resort town, spoiled only by the hustling of the realtors to turn it into a big and sprawling one; on my last visit, I'd overheard a waitress saying that the area was expected to become like another Palm Springs. I'd been split between mourning the passing of an old friend, and wondering if I'd be able to get the stake together to pick up a piece of land somewhere on the outskirts so that I could then sit back and watch its value climb. I counted up, and between my salary and my savings and my monthly outgoings the most that I could have afforded would have been a box number in the local Post Office.

We went for lunch in a place that I knew where we could sit out the back on a board terrace. Beyond the rail we could look out across Oak Creek, its valley sides lined with cypress and pine and rising to the rust-colored mesas that gave the area its name. Loretta didn't order much and said that she wasn't too hungry, but I could see that she was making an effort. Afterwards the two of them went out to see if they could pick up some swimwear in one of the main street shops, and I stayed behind at the table for a while.

Not for the first time, I wondered exactly what I was going to say to her.

I knew what I wanted to tell her, and that was the whole truth, from start to finish; but I was too aware of how it would sound, of how it was an open invitation to disbelief. I'd been out there and I'd looked Woods in the eyes and we'd known each other as enemies, but this wasn't the kind of knowledge that I felt I could pass on in words; the only way that I can describe it is to say that it was more part of the fabric, like when my old man died and changed my understanding of death from something that existed in the same layer of reality as taxes and airline schedules to something deeper and more permanent. Perhaps I could make up something that had a part of the truth in it but which sounded more plausible, but I wasn't sure that I could do the job. I'm not exactly what you'd call imaginative.

I was confident that this thing was going to work itself out, and that this was the best way to go about it; staying at

home would probably have meant a slide into a fearful
silence that would eventually become impossible to break.
And the one big bonus for me, the knowledge that made
every other problem seem small and manageable, was that
I'd found a cancer in the city and I'd cut it out. Maybe I'd
always have to stay an unsung hero, but at least I knew
what I'd done.

Or rather, I *thought* I knew.

I was soon to find out that I'd been wrong.

The place that I'd booked us into was about six miles
further on out of the town, and we headed there after lunch
to drop off our luggage. It was a small and inexpensive
motel called the Red Ridge Terrace, and there didn't seem
to be anybody around as we parked the jeep on its
stonechip forecourt and rang the bell outside the office for
attention. A friendly guy in his sixties appeared, apparently
from raking leaves around the back, and called for Jolene;
and moments later Jolene appeared from one of the units,
walking down towards us and shaking the office key out of
a bunch that hung beside her apron. Georgie went exploring
as we signed into the two adjacent rooms that I'd phoned
ahead and reserved for us, and then Loretta had to go and
find her when we'd moved the bags out of the jeep. Georgie
came trailing back behind her, insisting that she could
hardly believe it but she'd seen a *squirrel* go by not six feet
away. I told her that in Central Park, the squirrels formed
gangs and mugged the kids for money to buy peanuts.

After that we got back onto the road and went even
further into the valley, climbing and winding steeply
through the forest with little room for passing. The
roadside fruit stalls were all shuttered, and we passed a
number of campground access roads with barriers across
stencilled *Closed until April*. It suited me fine, I hate
crowds. I hate being one of them.

We left the car on a red-dirt strip by the road and spent a
couple of hours at Slide Rock, after which the three of us
went for a walk up the bed of a dry gulley. There had been a
lot of older kids splashing around at the Rock, but here we
saw nobody. The gulley had been sculpted and smoothed
into all kinds of weird shapes and steps, and we went as
high as we could until a fallen tree blocked our way. Then it

was everybody race back to the jeep, and back into town in search of the perfect deep-pan pizza.

Loretta was unwinding, one notch at a time; I could almost hear the clicks. Perhaps tonight, when Georgie was asleep, she'd be able to let her worries out for some exercise.

There was a message waiting for me at the Red Ridge; someone had been phoning during the afternoon, asking for me but leaving no name.

Loretta said, "Who knows we're here, Alex?"

"I left a number at the station desk in case they wanted to reach me," I explained. "I'm still on suspension, remember."

"Could it be trouble?"

"There's only one way to find out."

The pay phone was outside, under a shingled awning that ran the length of the units and provided a covered walkway down to a roofed lean-to area at the end of the building. It was now the last quarter of the sunset hour, where the greens go to black and the blues and reds turn vivid and metallic before dying away altogether. I shivered a little in the evening chill, wishing that I'd picked up a sweatshirt before I'd come out.

"This is Sergeant Volchak, District Five," I said when I finally got through on the office extension. "Has somebody been trying to get hold of me today?"

"Alex?" a voice said, and I recognised Blowjob Horowitz. "That you?"

"Yeah," I said, relaxing a little. "Who's been calling?"

"I don't know anything about that, but they sent somebody around to your house this afternoon with a letter. Woods has dropped out of sight and there's no complaint against you. Your suspension ends Monday."

"That's good news. Thanks."

"Wait until you see what you'll be walking into. It's been chaos here, all day."

"Why, what's happened?"

"You haven't heard? Go turn on the TV, it'll tell you more than I can. All I know is, this new boy makes the Encanto Park killer look like Mister Rogers."

90

When I got back to the rooms, Loretta was inside with Georgie and presumably helping her to get into her night things. She put her head out of the door as I went by, and said, "They tell you anything good?"

"I don't think so," I said, and went into the next unit.

There was a large black and white TV in the corner of my room, its aerial lead trailing up to a hole in the ceiling; I plugged it in and switched it on, and as it slowly warmed into life I found that the sound wasn't working. The volume switch turned too easily, not meeting the resistance that it should. The TV next door was working fine, because I could hear it through the wall, but I didn't want to walk in and explain to Georgie why I wanted her to change channels from *The 'A' Team* or whatever it was that she was being allowed to watch in the last half-hour or so before she'd be packed off to sleep. With a certain and formless apprehension, I watched as the monochrome image resolved itself into the main news story of the evening.

A plain house, with stuccoed walls painted in some medium tone – probably the dusty kind of blue that looked good on many of the houses on the south side of the city. There were portable barriers in the near foreground which I knew would have *Police Barrier – Do Not Cross* stencilled on them in much the same style as the campground notices that we'd passed earlier in the day, and beyond the barriers were enough official vehicles to spell *major disaster* clearly in my mind, sound or no sound. The coverage then cut to an unsteady hand-held shot on a long lens which showed stretchers with blankets draped full-length over the bodies that they carried, five of them emerging from the house in a sombre procession as the news people fought and jostled all around the camera to peek through the cars at the one narrow angle that would show them anything. Then, as there was a jump cut to a lot of our people getting into vehicles, I heard the door to the next unit open and close and then Loretta slipped in to join me. She was about to speak, but didn't; there's something in the coverage of a tragic aftermath that makes it instantly identifiable, so instead she came over and sat on the bed. I'd been sitting in near-darkness, and when she reached over to switch on the reading lamp the TV picture jumped and threatened to get smaller.

I could hear another station's commercials running on the set next door, and they made a weird counterpoint to the sight of Lieutenant Michaels walking by and shaking his head as a sudden forest of microphones and mini-recorders were thrust in from every side of the frame towards him. They supered his name at the bottom of the screen, and I wondered what they were saying about him. Then, another unsteady image, this time a sneak-shot around the back of the house; keeping newspeople back at a scene like this is always like trying to dam up a creek with sawdust, you stop them in one place and they just come through at another. The camera zoomed in on a ground-floor window, and then immediately they froze the frame to show that there was writing of some kind on the glass, and then they did some kind of electronic trick and flipped it around so that it read the way that it would when seen from inside the room.

It read

and whatever it had been written in, it had run.

After a few moments on the anchorman, they went into some archive footage. Loretta frowned at the old film and said, "Isn't that Manson?" and I made a noise of agreement as I stood up. Suddenly I had to go outside for a while.

The roofed lean-to at the back of the motel overlooked a terrace with two blackened barbecues and a couple of tables. It was now lit from above by a single naked bulb, around which moths were circling. I sat on one of the benches with my own weak shadow falling across the table in front of me. Somewhere in the RV park in the valley down below the terrace, a door slammed. After a couple of minutes, another shadow joined mine.

92

Loretta said, "You didn't kill him after all, did you?"

She sounded relieved. I said, "I took him out into the desert and shot him, but I didn't stop him. We just saw him make another entry in his resumé."

"You can't be sure of that."

"Yes, I can. He's showing off, now. He's wiped out an entire family just to prove that he's still in business. Those words on the glass, they were a message to me. He's dancing out of reach."

"So, how come no-one else is in on this? Why should you carry it alone?"

I looked at her now. The pale light showed up her lines, but it also stripped away the years. I said, "Do you like horror stories, Loretta?"

She became a little suspicious, reluctant. "Depends how close to home they are," she said.

"Well," I said, "then you're not going to like this one."

What I did then was to tell her the whole story from day one, step by step but with no conclusions or commentary; the idea was that I'd let her supply the connections for herself, go through it and see light in the same places that I'd seen it. Once you accepted the basic truth of the sequence, everything else had to fall into place.

Or so I hoped.

I didn't get to finish, because when I reached the part where I arrived home and found Georgie gone, the phone under the overhang started to ring. I tried to ignore it, thinking that someone else might come out and pick it up, but it carried on and I began to lose the competition with the distraction. I had to break off and go around the corner and answer it.

"This is the Red Ridge Motel's phone," I said. "Who's that?"

"Alex Volchak?" said a voice that I didn't know.

"Yes?"

"*Sergeant* Alex Volchak?" Whoever he was, he sounded young.

"Who *is* this?" I said.

"You weren't so hard to find," he said, and rang off.

15

Loretta had gone inside, and I could hear that she was putting Georgie to bed. I tapped lightly on her door and waited out on the boardwalk.

When she came out, I managed to smile and said, "Wrong number."

"It happens," she said.

"Yeah, I know. Now, listen . . ."

"Please, Alex," she said. "My head's spinning so much, I can hardly stand it. I don't know what to say."

I wanted to tell her that this was one of those things that's better not said out loud. But I could only shrug.

She said, "Let's talk in the morning, okay?"

"Sure," I said, and she went back inside. She hadn't given me a straight look in all the time she'd been out.

Back in my own room, I turned out my bag and took my service gun from under the spare shirts where I'd packed it. State law only allows for the carrying of unconcealed weapons, but over the years I'd developed a blind spot towards it and now I was glad that I had. I don't mind admitting it, I was deeply scared. I didn't know who he was now, or how he'd found me, or from how far away he'd phoned. He might be down in Phoenix still, or he might have been calling from a roadside pay phone only a couple of miles away. Whatever the case, I didn't know whether to run or to stay put or what.

I hefted the revolver, checked the load. I knew that the safety that it could buy me was strictly temporary, that I could kill him over and over and he could come back in new shapes and with new faces, but it was the only reassurance that I had to hold onto. Jesus, I felt small; there I'd been, thinking that I'd wiped him out, when all that I'd done had been to pull on the lion's tail. Now I could feel his dead breath as he turned on me, and I didn't know what I was going to do or how I could possibly handle this. I suppose I felt guilty about the people on the TV, but perhaps not as guilty as I should; I had my own to look after, and Loretta wasn't even with me in appreciating the scale of the problem yet.

Running in the dark didn't seem like a good idea. There was only the one narrow valley road, and he knew the jeep; we'd be like rats in a drainpipe even in daylight. Besides, I wasn't even sure that I could get her to haul Georgie out of bed and come along. She had to be sitting there and questioning my sanity right at this moment – after what I'd been telling her, I'd have been surprised if she hadn't. But I'd broken the story on the assumption that I'd have time to follow it up, and that time had now been wiped away.

A problem.

I spent the next ten minutes or so outside, checking all around the motel, and had to come to the conclusion that it was pretty well undefendable. There was forest on three sides and the valley road on the fourth, and Woods – or rather, whoever he was now – could easily walk in from any of them. First thing in the morning I'd have to come up with some bright idea about moving on to somewhere else, and I'd have to sound casual about it in case Loretta should pick up the signals; and in the meantime, I'd simply have to sit awake with my door slightly open and my revolver on my knees, ready for action at the first sign of a prowler.

He'd turned the tables on me. I couldn't say that I liked it.

I set the room up with my chair by the window. If anybody came by, I'd hear his tread on the boardwalk and I'd be able to look out without hardly moving. I could see myself in the glass; the reflected spill of the reading lamp was green, and it didn't flatter me. I looked like somebody who'd been pulled out of the sea after a couple of days. I got a cup of lousy coffee from the two-cup courtesy maker in the bathroom, and paused to switch off the lamp as I carried it over to the chair.

Loretta's light went off after an hour, and just past midnight the outside lights went off as well. In that time I'd been in a more or less constant state of tension, screwed up a little tighter evey time a car or a pickup turned in onto the forecourt and new people checked in for the night. But couples and families were okay, it was loners who interested me. I went out a couple of times in response to sounds that I couldn't identify, and on one of them saw a cat with half a tail scoot across and down into the juniper trees.

I didn't think that I'd ever sleep on such a night. But it turned out that I was wrong.

I knew it the moment that I opened my eyes and saw daylight, and felt the aching stiffness in my neck and my back from sitting too long without shifting. My gun hand in my lap felt as if the wrist had been broken. What woke me was the sound of the early starters revving their engines outside, a sound enough to shake the thin walls as they warmed up and turned around on the forecourt. I squinted out of the window and saw the side of a red pickup going past, and then as the tail of the pickup cleared the way I could see that the slot where the jeep had been the night before was now empty.

My door, which I'd left open about six inches, was now closed. It must have been done gently, in order not to disturb me. I threw it open and rushed out, feeling as if all of my joints had been packed with gravel, my gun still in my hand and me not caring who saw it. Loretta and Georgie's room was empty, the linen stripped from the beds and folded neatly for collection. On the bedside table were a folded note with my name on it, and some change.

The note was an apology. The change, a contribution to my bus fare.

I got a ride into town with a couple who were in the area looking for a retirement home. I had to share the back seat with their dog, a little beach ball of an animal which made a sound like farting when it breathed and which farted every now and again just to show that it knew the difference. They dropped me in the uptown area before they turned off towards the newer developments to the west, and I walked over to where I could pick up the Greyhound service on its way down from Flagstaff. I had my bag in my hand and the gun stuck into my windcheater where I could get at it in a hurry if I needed to. I was lucky, I didn't have much more than half an hour to wait before the bus came through.

I picked up a copy of the *Republic* from a stand outside, and spent the time reading what it had to say about the slayings. The picture of the window-writing was reproduced, and the comparisons with the Manson family were repeated, but other than the names of the victims I didn't learn anything new save that Lieutenant Michaels had responded to a neighbor's call and had been the first one into the house. The actual details of what had gone on inside were, apparently, being withheld. This was standard, not least as a means of screening out the crank calls and confessions that would inevitably follow.

The bus was half-empty, and pulled out on time. I sat in a window seat and watched the road behind us, but nobody seemed to be following. I was the only passenger here who was sitting alone. I liked being a passenger of any kind about as much as I liked being in a crowd.

Loretta must have been awfully stealthy in making her getaway like that. The idea hurt a little, even though I could understand why she'd done it; I suppose that her leaving the bus fare was the part that had really got under my skin. The note itself had said a lot less. I think more than anything, I must have scared her; I'd been one of the few people in a strange town that she'd come to like and trust, and then suddenly I'd whipped off the rubber mask to reveal Mad Alex, the paranoid cop with the wacky delusions. But perhaps a little time away from me would change that, when she thought it over and realised that I hadn't told her anything that couldn't be checked for accuracy, with the exception of that one incident in the alley behind the gay bar which, as far as I knew, still hadn't been uncovered. She might think that the sequence led into madness, but it was a destination she'd sighted without any help from me.

If she thought about it at all. I also had to face the possibility that the shutters might slam down and stay down; although that wouldn't make the two of them any less of a target.

We were about midway between Cordes Junction and Black Canyon City, both of them big names attached to little places that appeared to be out in the middle of nowhere, when I heard one of the people further down the bus saying something about "a jeep turned over". I stood up quickly and looked out, but I couldn't see anything; but then, everybody else was looking out of the other side, and when I slid over into a spare seat opposite what I saw in the receding distance was enough to send me forward to the driver.

"Stop the bus," I said.

He glanced at me once, briefly, a quick flash of my own image in his aviator sunglasses. He was about fifty, in his shirtsleeves, and looked as if he'd been put together out of rock and sandpaper and wire. He said, "What?"

"Something's happening back there, you have to let me off."

He didn't look at me again. "Regulations won't allow it. Will you go back to your seat, please?"

"Screw the regulations, this is police business."

"So, where's your ID? Back to your seat." And then, almost an afterthought: "Please."

I reached into my windcheater and pulled out the gun and held it up in front of him where he couldn't help but see it. I didn't point it at him or anything, just showed him the side view and said, "Is this ID enough for you?"

It got the fast result that I wanted; somebody further back in the bus shrieked, and immediately he hit the brakes and I had to grab at one of the chrome bars to stay on my feet. The doors were open before we'd even come to a stop, and as I jumped out they closed again so fast that they almost bit me. The bus kept on rolling, not waiting around in case I should change my mind, and seconds later I was standing in its dust. My last view was of three open-mouthed black faces in the rear window.

I was now about a mile further on from where I wanted to be, so I started to walk along the shoulder of the road where it was beginning to crumble into the soft stuff. Within the first hundred yards I passed a dented silver mailbox at the end of a dirt road, and that was the only sign of habitation that I saw which didn't have four wheels and go zipping by well in excess of the legal limit. Not, that is, until I looked up into the sky and saw a helicopter in the livery of the Arizona Department of Public Safety passing low overhead and dropping to set down close to the spot by the road where a Renegade jeep lay belly-up with a County vehicle and a DPS cruiser alongside it. I started to run, but I was still some distance away. I saw people in white hopping out, bending low as the blades still turned, and I was only just leaving the road and starting out across the scrub as the copter took aboard its load and revved up to lift again. The patrolmen on the ground held onto their hats as the machine climbed into the air, turned around its own centre, and dipped its nose for extra lift and speed as it began the valley run down into Phoenix.

There were two of them waiting for me, a patrolman of the DPS and a man from the Yavapai County Sheriff's Office. They were admirably laid-back about my approach, both of them smiling lazily and letting me see the pump-action shotguns before they levelled them to cover me.

"You want to stop and raise your hands?" the DPS man said, and the Deputy said, "I'd advise it."

Obviously the Greyhound driver had radioed in a report on my unorthodox exit from his bus, and word had travelled fast. I stood with my hands in the air as the DPS man came around to frisk me from behind as the Deputy kept me covered. I felt the weight of the revolver go first, and then my wallet from my back pocket.

I said, "I'm Sergeant Alex Volchak, Phoenix PD."

"He is, too," the DPS man said with some surprise as he came around the front again, my wallet open in his hand. It didn't seem to change anything, just an Interesting Fact to spice up the encounter.

The Deputy said, "You gave some people quite a scare back there. Radio's been buzzing ever since."

"I was in a hurry," I said. "What happened here?"

He glanced back at the overturned jeep, which didn't seem to be too much damaged. There was a dirt sideroad with a built-up banking a few yards further on, where fresh tyre scars indicated the start of the roll. I didn't have to look twice to know that it was Loretta's. I'd been hoping that the color might be a coincidence, but I'd been wrong.

He said, "Tell you what. You talk, and *we'll* listen."

I let my hands fall, and nobody complained. I said, "Her

99

name's Loretta Heilbron and her daughter's name is Georgina. She's a widow. We came up for a couple of days in the canyon, the Red Ridge Motel. Last night we had a disagreement, this morning she set off without me. That's why I had to get the bus."

The Deputy looked at the DPS man. They were both about twenty-four, twenty-five, and still looked pretty fresh. He said, "What do you think?"

"Sounds solid enough to me," the patrolman said. "But I'm inclined to hang onto the hardware for a while. At least, as long as the Sergeant's so jumpy."

"Keep it as long as you like," I said, "I've got others. Just tell me what I missed."

The Deputy returned his shotgun to his car. "We've got a witness says the car was forced off the road by another vehicle," he said. "Something beat-up, blue, and foreign is the best description we can get. It cut across in front of the jeep and forced it onto the dirt road, then got in behind and pushed. Driver couldn't hold it straight, so the jeep rolled off the rise. No safety belt."

"How bad is it?"

"Bad. A lot of things broken."

"She was still conscious when I got here," the DPS man added, "but she wasn't making a lot of sense."

I could see what must have happened. He'd have seen the jeep and assumed that we'd all be together. He might have been waiting down the road from the motel. Loretta wouldn't have suspected a damn thing if she hadn't believed me anyway.

I said, "What about the little girl?"

The two men exchanged a glance.

"There was no little girl," the patrolman said. "The woman was alone."

16

They made a radio check and told me that the helicopter had taken Loretta to the Lincoln Samaritan hospital in the north-west of the city. The patrolman had to wait around for his incident team to arrive and start taking photographs and measurements, but the Deputy gave me a ride down to the nearest truck stop so that I could ask around for someone to take me the rest of the way. They let me have my gun back, as well. Technically it was now up to the bus company if they wanted to pursue the matter – I had, after all, identified myself as a police officer before showing the revolver, and showing it was all that I'd done . . . no pointing, no threatening, just a hurried attempt to establish my identity at a time of emergency.

It was bullshit and we all knew it, but it would probably get me by.

He took me as far as Rock Springs, just short of the county line, where he flagged down a silver-blue Fury that had a loosely bouncing trunk lid. The driver was in stained kitchen whites, and before he got out I saw him slip on a little paper hat as if to say Hey, I'm a working guy too. The result of the negotiation was that the driver got a warning but no coupon in return for taking me on to the hospital. He drove all the way from there at a steady fifty, and I don't think that we exchanged more than four words in all of that time.

The Lincoln Samaritan was a new hospital, built right out on the northern edge of town to serve the expanding fringe of the city. I walked in the wrong door and couldn't find my way, but was eventually directed towards the surgical facility. Loretta was still in the operating room, I was told by the nurse on desk duty, but I was welcome to wait around. I didn't know whether to take this as good news or bad. Now that I knew she'd come through the helicopter lift, I had to wonder what kind of mess she was in. A part of me didn't even want to be told.

There was a little waiting area with low chairs and unread magazines. I got a coffee from the machine, set it down, and forgot all about it.

I had to face the possibility that he'd taken Georgie. I only hoped that he was bright enough to see that she'd be of more use to him safe and in one piece; maimed and dead, she'd be useless as bait or leverage. If he'd taken her. There could be some other explanation, but I sat there and I tried and I couldn't come up with one.

Where had I gone wrong?

After a while, I wandered back over to the desk. The nurse on station, a trim-looking middle-aged woman, gave me a smile. Things seemed quiet, so it seemed like a good time to get her to talk. I'd already let her know that I was with the police. When it's likely to help, I try to work it into the conversation early.

I said, "I've got a weird question for you."

"We get 'em all the time," she said.

"Say you get somebody brought in dead, and suddenly his eyes open and he's okay. Maybe a guy who'd had an accident, something like a shock that stopped his heart but didn't damage him much. Would that be unusual enough to be news?"

"No," she said.

"It wouldn't?"

"Nobody here's dead until they get a certificate. Nobody gets a certificate until the medical staff have used up every trick they know. We get people right on the brink, practically shaking hands with the angels, and still we pull them back. Not every day, but it happens."

I decided to go for broke. "How about three days ago, early in the afternoon."

She didn't have to think for more than a moment. "No," she said. "I was here, it was a quiet shift. What's your interest?"

"Just academic. Say somebody down in the morgue climbed out of his drawer and disappeared. Wouldn't that be news?"

"That would be a George Romero movie, and *I'd* be on the first plane out of here."

But it was something worth pursuing. After being told that it would be another hour or more before they'd be able to tell me anything about Loretta's condition, I spent the next thirty minutes trying to get the loan of a pool car for the afternoon out of one of the hospital's administrative officers. It was like trying to dig a pebble out of a lump of set concrete, but in the end I managed it. I drove into nearby Peoria and picked up one of those giveaway magazines that are actually thinly veiled ads for new housing developments; what I really wanted was the list of all the valley's hospitals and their services that I found under the heading of 'Caring for our Lives'. I could have found the basics in the phone book, but this way I got all the background and a map as well.

I was away from the Lincoln Samaritan for more than the hour. When I got back, Loretta was out.

I had to wait around a while longer for the doctor to come out and talk to me; in the absence of any immediate kin, I'd have to suffice. This high-school kid in glasses had taken my arm and was hustling me down the Surgical corridor before I belatedly realised that *this* was the doctor.

"Okay," he said. "She's conscious, but she's well-doped. Tell her she's doing fine, tell her she's still got her looks, and then get yourself out of there."

They'd wheeled her out into a low-lit recovery room prior to transfer to the intensive care unit. I saw sheets and IVs and machines and, almost as an incidental in the middle of it all, one fragile but recognisable form. They'd fixed her in some kind of body brace that immobilised her head.

I crouched down alongside her. "Loretta?" I said softly. "You hear me?"

She took a moment to respond, like somebody swimming up from the depths.

"Nick?" she said.

"It's Alex, Loretta. Don't try to turn your head." Now that I was closer, I could see the silver screws that were holding the arrangement in place like a crown. I moved around a little so that she'd be able to see me.

"Alex?" she said. "I'm sorry."

"That's okay."

"He found us. I think he'd been waiting. He followed us all the way down."

I said, "Did you get a look at him?"

For a moment I thought she hadn't heard, but then she said, "You were right. I couldn't believe it, but you were. He had a different face, but it was him. He'd thought you were in the jeep, and then he thought you were trying to make a fool of him because you weren't. You've scared him, Alex."

"Scared him how?"

"He stood over me and he kept asking, how much does he know?" And then she frowned, as her doped memory dredged up something new. "Then he said he was going to take Georgie . . . did he, Alex? Did he take her?"

"No," I said, feeling ashamed of myself. "No, he didn't."

"Thank God," she said, closing her eyes. She was as pale as the sheet beneath her, and I could see a blue pulse of life beating at her temple. "Is she hurt?"

"She's fine," I said.

Loretta opened her eyes and looked at me again, and I was afraid that she'd be able to see right through my lie; but the pain and the drugs had clouded what was normally so sharp, and she only said, "Don't bring her here. I don't want her to see me like this. Tell her . . . think of something to tell her, Alex."

"I will," I said.

God Almighty, I was thinking as I walked away. Solid silver.

Imagine the *bill*.

17

I found what I was looking for midway through the afternoon at the Tempe Community Hospital on Mill Avenue, barely three blocks from the cheap hotel where I'd left Woods his little surprise. I'd done a couple of the uptown hospitals before I'd thought to come down here, because it had taken me a while to realise that once he'd flown and found his refuge gone, there might be some kind of limit on the time he could spend and the distance he could cover before coming up with an alternative. I mean, just because he was something that I'd never come across before, it didn't mean that he could ignore the natural laws that the rest of us lived by. He wasn't God, he couldn't be everywhere at once.

His name was Bob Winter, and he was a sophomore student on some kind of land studies course at the State University. He'd been rushed into the Emergency Room after taking a steep dive into the wrong end of a swimming pool; after cracking his head on the tiles, he'd been floating face-down with his lungs full of water when the lifeguard had reached him. They'd pumped him out on the poolside, and a paramedic had forced oxygen into him from a breather-bag during the short ride to the ER. As they'd been running him up the ramp, he'd suddenly opened his eyes and started to cough up chlorine.

This, as far as I could work out the timing from the ER log, had been about four minutes after my hunting rifle had practiced a little cranial surgery of its own on Woods. Not bad going. Winter had immediately established himself as a problem patient, refusing to give his name and demanding his clothes; it was only when these were sent along from the pool that they were able to find out who he was. It was a telling detail, as far as I was concerned; he couldn't give them a name because he didn't know it himself. When he made a transfer, all he got was the body – its skills and its memories having died with the owner. He'd have to go through his own pockets just to find out where home was.

Damn his luck.

I got an address for Winter, a room in a student residence on the Tyler Mall. I was half-ready for trouble, but I really didn't expect him still to be around.

I can't remember when I last saw so many bicycles. Car parking was on the outside fringe of the campus so I had to walk the rest of the way in along a palm-shaded boulevard. I felt really conspicuous, even though nobody paid me any particular attention; it was just kids flocking from one place to another or sitting around on the grass. Maybe it wouldn't have been such a bad place for him to hide out after all; he could have seen me coming a mile away.

But no, I knew him better than that. He was a loner, and this was all too public. He'd have flown; but at least I might get a clue as to where.

I found his room up on the fourth floor of the residential block and knocked on his door. The corridor was all new wood and exposed brick, with maroon-colored carpet tiles on the floor; it was fairly hushed apart from somebody's sound system playing a few doors away. I knocked again, but it was clear that nothing was going to happen, so I moved along and tried next door.

I disturbed a curly young guy and his girlfriend, but they'd obviously been going at their books rather than at each other so I didn't feel too bad about it. They were both shoeless, and came out to talk to me rather than letting me in.

"I'm looking for Bob," I explained. "Is he around?"

"Nobody knows," the boy said. "He was in an accident a couple of days ago, and I think it shook him up."

"That's why I'm here. Has he been acting strangely, or what?"

"We found him downstairs, that same evening. It was like he knew he lived here, but he couldn't remember the layout. But then we brought him upstairs, and he was fine."

I'd have bet that he was. I could imagine him getting his

bearings, playing a part, fooling people. After all, he'd been doing it almost forever.

The girl added, "Then he went in his room and closed the door, and we haven't seen him since."

"Except in the parking lot. That time he was trying all the cars with his keys, like he couldn't even remember which one was his. It was scary to watch. Like another person altogether. We went straight to the medical center to tell them about it and they said for us to bring him over, but after that he never came back."

I said, "What kind of car does he drive?"

"A blue Toyota," the boy said. "He calls it Joshua. Are you with student welfare?"

"My name's Alex Volchak," I said. "I'm with the police department. Your friend could be in some danger. He walked out of the hospital against advice and he never even signed a waiver."

"Is *that* all they're worried about . . ?" the boy began, but I raised my hand in a calm-down gesture.

"Of course it isn't," I said. "Have you any idea where he might have gone to?"

He glanced at the girl, either for inspiration or reassurance. "I don't know of anywhere. This is where he lived. His family are all halfway around the world, somewhere . . . something to do with the diplomatic service. I don't know that he could locate them in a hurry, let alone join them."

I said, "Any way that we could take a look in his room?"

I was expecting suspicion and evasion – it's almost an article of faith with a lot of college kids to regard the police as natural enemies, until they get mugged or have something stolen – but what I got here was more reluctance. Seeing Bobby Winter with a demon on the inside had disturbed them both deeply, although of course they didn't know the real reason why.

The boy said, "I don't see how. He left the door locked."

"And since when did a locked door count for anything in a student hall?"

There was a flicker of a masked response in his eyes then. He hesitated for a moment, but then he said, "Give me five minutes."

He went back into his room, leaving me out in the

corridor with the girl. She was nice-looking and freckled, and looked as if she might get fat one day if she didn't watch herself. There was an embarrassed silence for a while as she tried to think of something to say, and what finally came out was, "You want a coffee, or something?"

"No, thanks," I said.

"This *is* just a welfare thing, isn't it? I mean . . . Bob hasn't done anything else, has he?"

"You think he might have?"

"I don't know. Before the accident, I'd have said no . . ."

"Was there something specific that happened?" I pressed her. "Something he did, something he said?"

Further down the corridor, a door opened and closed. Rock music surged for a second, then shut off again. She said, "He did say something," and she looked at her bare feet and the floor, starting to blush a little. "We were standing right here and he asked me to come back later, on my own. Kind of leaned over and whispered it, so Jack couldn't hear. I mean, Bob's a *nice* guy. He knows how it is with Jack and me. Why'd he say a thing like that?"

I wouldn't have cared to dwell on what might have happened to her if she'd taken him up on his offer. I said, "A bang on the head can mess people up. Does Jack know about this?"

"No," she said quickly. "And please don't tell him, either."

"Trust me." I looked at the door behind her, which was still closed. "What's he doing in there?"

"There's a panel in the back of the closet, it unscrews and comes right out. Lets you straight through into the next room. They're always in and out of each others' places, playing jokes and setting booby-traps."

As she was saying this, Bobby Winter's door opened right on cue and the curly kid called Jack appeared. He looked as if he'd been preparing a smile of triumph and it had been knocked right out of him.

He said, "I don't believe this."

He stepped back, pulling the door all the way open so that we could follow him inside. It was a narrow single room with a washbasin behind the door, a desk over at the window, and a bed and storage cupboards along the wall in between; the whole place had been taken apart, everything pulled out of the drawers and thrown around and the books swept down from the shelves.

"His tape player's gone," Jack said. "And his TV."

"Any chance that anyone else may have done this?" I said.

"They'd have to go through my room to get in. And I'd know."

I looked over at the closet, straight through into a mirror-image of the room on the other side, except that the image was neat and empty. It made me think of some book that I'd read as a kid, whose title I couldn't remember. The tape player and the TV, I'd no doubt, would now be in a pawnshop somewhere. If Bobby Winter had kept any savings stashed, it was also probable that the new Bobby Winter had found them.

I said, "Listen. I'm on the case, okay? Don't worry about it. I want to find a photograph, but we'll leave everything else as it is. It's no crime to mess up your own stuff."

They both looked around doubtfully, but they didn't argue. They were troubled by this fierce inburst of chaos into their otherwise regulated and protected lives, and I was the voice of order telling them that the world was still a safe place to be. And I didn't want them asking awkward questions that might lead to some official departmental follow-up – Winter might get to hear of it, and then the trail might be broken again.

We found a photograph, showing Winter with two younger sisters. He was dark, thin, bookish, nothing remarkable about him at all. He wore glasses and a smile in the picture; go outside into the Mall and throw a stick, and you could probably hit a dozen like him.

As I was leaving, Jack said, "I just hope he's safe. He's a good friend."

I looked once at the girl, said nothing, and left them to get on with putting the closet back together.

18

I walked across the street from the campus and into a coffee shop where I could see they had a phone, and from there I rang the hospital for an update on Loretta's condition. As I waited to be put through, I turned to look behind me; I seemed to have this constant sensation of being watched, even when nobody was looking my way. The shop's counters were lined with students, books open and heads down, most with only coffee or a glass of water. A bearded kid with a philosophy text propped before him was muttering "Shit, shit," as he flicked through the pages of his notebook. Further down the same counter, a silent girl was going through a new hardcover book and scoring through some of its lines with a yellow magic marker.

Now, there was a point. Every body that he'd taken so far had been male. Was that out of preference, or out of necessity?

The desk nurse for the intensive care unit came through. I gave her my enquiry.

"Mrs Heilbron was stable until half an hour ago," she told me, "when she began to haemmorhage. She's having another emergency operation now. Are you a relative?"

"No."

"Then I really can't give you any more than that. We've managed to contact next of kin and they're on their way."

"It's as bad as that?"

"I'm sorry. Perhaps you can speak to Mister Heilbron when he arrives."

There was a silence while I took that one in.

Then I said, "Yeah . . . I'll call again. Thanks."

I dropped the car back at the hospital, but I didn't go in. I called a cab and then waited around outside for it to arrive and take me home. I was in a daze; part of it was that I hadn't eaten since the previous night, but I couldn't even think of facing anything now. I'd found the trail again, taken it as far as I could – which had been to a ransacked room in a student hall, and no further.

I'd pulled the lion's tail, all right, but he'd done more than turn on me . . . he was taking my whole world apart, one piece at a time, and I couldn't even see where he was coming from.

The cabbie asked me if I wanted him to go a couple of blocks off the route so that I could see the 'massacre house'. I said no, thanks, and he shrugged and turned up his radio.

I paid him off at the gates of the trailer site, and walked in alone.

Woods, Winter, what was the difference. He was smoke, I couldn't fight him or beat him. I'd tried, and Loretta and Georgie had paid for my mistake; now there didn't seem to be anything more that I could do other than to sit around and wait for him to come. How many other innocents would have to suffer as part of the show before he decided to move in and deliver the final stroke, I didn't know. I'd have to put on the uniform again and go through the motions, but I felt as if the dying had already started, there on the inside.

A white car was waiting alongside my trailer, parked across the end of my own. So soon? I remember thinking as I stopped in the middle of the gravel road, and the door of the car opened.

Lieutenant Michaels got out. He was in uniform, and on duty. He said, "Alex? You look wrecked."

"Got it in one," I said.

"Alone?"

"Right."

"I called the motel and they said you'd checked out this morning. I've been stopping by on and off for the last two hours."

"I already heard about the letter," I said, making a move towards the house, but Michaels was shaking his head.

"It's not about the letter," he said. "Get in the car."

I stopped. "To go where?"

"I'll explain on the way."

"Don't I even get five minutes to change?"

"No," he said.

I got in. What could I say? The mood I was in, anybody could have ordered me around. I'd known Michaels for about five years and I'd even been to his house once, but our relationship had always been professional rather than personal. Now, as we drove out towards his district within which my own squad area fell, he was giving nothing away.

We made a turn onto a quiet street. I recognised it straight away as the street on which the 'massacre house' stood; the street was still blocked by barriers and there were some tall screens around the house itself, but a young probationary policewoman ducked to see into the car and then moved a barrier back so that we could pass. Michaels cruised by slowly, and then picked up speed as we left at the other end of the street. Apart from keeping some attention on the road, he'd been watching me all the time. I'd been tense, nothing I could help, and now he must have seen me relax a little.

He said, "You thought that was where we were going?"

"If this is some kind of stunt," I said, "I wish you'd get to the point of it."

"No stunt. We're going to a murder scene, but not that one. You think you've had a heavy day, wait until you see these people."

Something was wrong with Michaels. It hadn't been too noticeable at first, but as time went on I began to see that he was edgy and disturbed in a way that I'd never seen in him before. He wouldn't say where we were going; and after the second attempt, I gave up trying to get it from him.

It was only after another forty-five minutes, slowed by the late-afternoon traffic, that I found out.

By then we'd travelled all the way across the city and were coming over the hills into the select north-eastern quarter where the rich people lived; I mean, the kind of people so rich that they could buy one of those places on the lower slopes of the Camelback Mountains and then not even bother to live in it for most of the year. It was an area that I only really knew as a tourist; I'd brought dates up here to the Camelback Inn for drinks a few times, when I'd really wanted to impress them, but that was about my only connection.

When we made the turn into a long private road I realised that we weren't aiming for an individual house, but for one of those walled developer villages near to the country club. This one was mostly screened by new trees and bushes, with only barred windows or garage doors peeking through. I couldn't see what we were doing here; it was way out of our area, after all.

The guard at the main gate took a look and then waved us through, as if we were expected. We didn't get more than fifty yards before we had to stop at the tail-end of a jam of police and County vehicles, and it was here that Michaels switched off the engine and got out. I followed, looking around. It was my first time actually inside a place like this, and I was curious. The architect had obviously had a Mediterranean concept in mind, a little piece of Renaissance Italy re-drafted for the tastes of local money so that the final effect was of a quiet corner in Disneyland. We walked around by a big fountain that splashed away as the centerpiece of the main plaza, and climbed a rock path with a white stone bell tower marking its end. I knocked on the stone as I passed, and it was hollow.

Michaels looked back at me. "Hey," he said, "come on."

I shrugged and said, "I don't get it."

"Simple. He didn't only hit one house, he hit two. Only for this one he got past a wall and private guards and dog patrols without being seen, and he got out again the same way. Kind of determined for an opportunist, wouldn't you say?"

Winter had been *here*? "Jesus," I said. 'Who'd he hit?"

But Michaels carried on.

I suppose it was cleverly laid out, if you go for that kind of thing. From each rambling white villa all that you could see was the roof of any other, and then not too close. The greenery was dense and well-planned, and keeping it in condition must have been a full-time job for a squad of gardeners. I could imagine it at night; they'd probably floodlight it in reds and greens, and the transplanted palms would move gently in the evening air. That's how they did it around the Camelback Inn, anyway. I didn't care for it much myself, but it had always impressed my dates.

I could hear the buzz before we even came up out of the bushes. Then we came up level with the terrace, and there we were.

There must have been at least four separate incident teams in and around the house, all climbing over one another and all of them arguing. There were some of our own people that I recognised, and others that I didn't know at all. We stood out on the terrace and waited as Michaels sent a message inside. I tried to see in through the full-length windows, but it was smoky glass and all that I could make out were moving shapes. I could only think of one reason why I should be here, which was that Winter might have left some deliberate clue or pointer involving me. If he had, it couldn't be anything too definite or they'd have done rather more than send Michaels alone to collect me. I wondered what I'd say, when faced with it.

We were there for about ten minutes before Berman came out; he was Chief of Detectives, young in the job but fairly well-respected by those who reckoned they knew what they were talking about. He looked from Michaels to me, and said, "Alex Volchak?"

"That's me," I said.

"Come inside, there's something I want you to take a look at. Don't worry, we already moved the bodies out."

I suppose it wouldn't have looked quite as bad if the big lounge hadn't been so all-over white; the plaster walls, the wool carpet, even the furniture was white leather. It looked as if somebody had dynamited a live pig in the middle of it all. We walked through across rubber sheets, a makeshift path that kinked in the middle to avoid a particularly nasty stain with a body-shape taped out around it. The shape, which was sexless like they always are, wasn't too big.

Three steps led us into a tiled passage running all the way down the side of the house, and the walls here were unmarked except for a single fading line that looked as if it might have been painted on by a sputtering aerosol. It was like a signpost, pointing us towards the room at the end of the passage.

This turned out to be part-office, part-den, with a big desk and a couple of filing cabinets and a bookcase full of Readers' Digest Condensed Books that didn't even look as if they'd been opened. There was more mess on the desktop, spread all over the papers and ledgers there, and this time the tape showed an outline of someone slumped forward with his arms outstretched. It reminded me of those blast-shadows they found on a wall at Hiroshima. There were a lot of people standing around in here, most of them apparently with nothing to do, and all of them talking and pointing here and there.

Berman eased around behind the desk. "You can thank the air conditioning that the smell isn't worse," he said, addressing me and Michaels equally. "They might have been lying around here for even longer if it wasn't for sightseers up on the mountain getting a glimpse of the body in the pool."

I was looking at the wall behind him; the big hanging map there told me in an instant why I'd been brought over. Apart from the colored pins which clustered in the part of the map corresponding to the downtown area of the city, its most eyecatching feature was the runny, handwritten legend

and just below this in the desert, a large, bloody cross. The cross was an approximation of the place where I'd scooped out a shallow grave for the body of Woods and then covered it over with stones.

Berman said, "Any comments?"

"No," I said cagily. "What can I say? I don't even know whose place this is."

"Jeff Miransky," he said, looking at the spot where the body had been as if there was still some after-trace of the physical presence lingering there. "Small-time thief turned big-time businessman, among other things the part-owner of the Paradise Motel. I'm looking for connections, Alex, and I'll grab a straw until something better comes along. The Paradise made news and you were there. Start thinking for me, will you?"

And it was as simple as that.

We were led out through the kitchen, being told to step carefully over a single female's shoe that lay with a chalk circle drawn around it. We came out by the surprisingly small pool, which was in the process of being drained so that its filters could be checked, and were pointed towards a spot on the other side of the outdoor furniture where the bushes had been pulled back and a section of the fence behind lifted away to give access over onto the patio of the next house along. This, it seemed, had become some kind of overspill and marshalling area in response to the awkwardness of the site and the widespread nature of the murder scene.

Seated at a white aluminium table at the end of the patio, with a kingsized piece of ham and a couple of tubs of coleslaw between them, were Morrell and McKay, the two Drug Squad detectives.

"Hey," Morrell said as they saw us, "the team's complete."

"It's the Paradise reunion," McKay added. "Grab a seat and eat."

Michaels stared at the food as if he couldn't quite believe that what he was seeing was real, and said, "How'd you get hold of that?"

"We raided the fridge," McKay said, gesturing shamelessly towards the villa behind him. "Just about everybody in the estate got up and ran when they heard the bad news, so nobody's home."

"And mayhem always gives me an appetite," Morrell added. "Join us?"

I hesitated for a moment. Then I said, "Yeah, I think I will."

"Oh, shit," Michaels said dully, and wandered away.

I pulled over a chair. I hadn't eaten at all since the previous night, and hadn't even given it a thought until this moment; now it all seemed to have caught up with me,

116

oddly sharpened and intensified by what I'd just seen. I could see what Morrell meant about mayhem, just as surely as Michaels couldn't; he wandered over to the house and stood looking in, deliberately doing his best not to see us.

I said, "So how come you're both here?"

"Same reason as you," Morrell said. "We're supposed to be sitting here in earnest discussion to see if we can come up with any connection between Apocalypse Now over there and what we saw at the Paradise Motel."

"You know of one?"

"No, 'cept that there's two people sitting at this table called Alex," (at this, McKay meekly raised a hand) "which is probably what made it worth a shot."

I said, "How long do you think they'll make us stick around? I've got things I have to do."

"Yeah," McKay agreed. "The whole point about being a cop is that you don't sit around like Joe Citizen waiting to be told what happens next."

Morrell handed me a Diet Pepsi. "What did you make of it in there?" he said.

I could sense a change in their attitude then, a shift to a more watchful mode; they might *look* like burned-out hippies, but they were still detectives, after all.

So I simply said, "It was bad."

"They say that the house on the park was worse," McKay said.

"No kidding?"

"And Michaels was the first one in." He glanced over at Michaels, who had wandered down to the far end of the pool and was well out of earshot. "You heard the story?"

"Only what they wrote in the newspaper."

"That was only half of it. Word is that he heard a kid screaming, so he went in without waiting for backup. Got the full effect in technicolor."

Morrell said, "Did he say what he saw?"

"No, but look at him. Half his mind's been somewhere else ever since. And I know Michaels, he isn't soft – whatever he saw, it must have been something that could frighten the crap out of a commode."

We sat around for a while longer, until it was clear that

we'd been forgotten, and then Morrell went through the fence to see if he could get a ruling on whether or not we should still hang around. We'd all agreed – Michaels excepted, because he hadn't even participated – that we couldn't come up with anything to throw light onto the mystery here.

Returning, Morrell said, "Somebody's out looking at the desert from a helicopter. See if they can't spot what the X is supposed to be marking."

"What about us?" McKay wanted to know.

"We're no use to anybody, we can go. They'll send for us if they need any more of our advice."

McKay looked at what was left on the table, which wasn't much apart from a hambone and some empty cola cans.

"I'll advise them all they like," he said. "It beats working any day."

I finally got home about eight, to find a rental car with its trunk open in the spot where Loretta usually parked her jeep. I went inside and, as I looked through my mail – the letter from the department about the lifting of my suspension and the probability of a written reprimand going into my file, and a second letter from Doctor Mulholland – I could hear the goings-on next door. I heard an older woman's voice saying, plaintively, *Well if she isn't here, where* is *she?* and a man's voice replying, *I don't know, Clara, I just don't know.* It should have occurred to me earlier that the Mister Heilbron mentioned by the receptionist wouldn't be Loretta's husband, but her father-in-law and Georgie's grandfather. I went through and dropped wearily onto the bed, and wondered what the hell I was going to do next.

And that was my day.

118

19

It was strange to put on the uniform again and go out to work; it felt like an unreal existence, a masquerade. Most people on the station seemed pleased to see me back, and the union representative took me aside and tried to sell me on the idea of making a claim for wrongful suspension, which I said I'd think about just so that I could get rid of him. I sat well to the back of the room at the start-of-shift meeting, where I learned that I was to lose four men from my squad to assist in the murder investigation whilst the rest of us would have to spread a little more thinly to cover the normal patrols. Michaels was also being attached to the murder investigation, as a kind of go-between to carry out essential liaison between the two areas' forces. *Because he's been fucking useless for anything else ever since*, I heard someone close by me mutter, and I looked across at Michaels. His uniform looked as if it had been slept in, although from his eyes it didn't look as if he'd slept at all. He also seemed oblivious to the unease that he was creating around himself.

For a moment I began to wonder whether . . . but no, it was too much to hope. He'd seen a bad sight to end all bad sights, but I was the only one who'd nosed out the truth about Woods/Winter. As we all rolled out, the KOOL-TV copter passed low overhead to pick up some footage of the patrol cars rolling out in force, regardless of the fact that most of us were going to be out covering ordinary duties. The press had been given a detailed release on the second murder in time for the late news the previous evening, and now they were all preparing their specials. They love anything like this, it's only natural. I sometimes wonder if they don't sit at home and pray for disasters when things get quiet.

I was hoping that I'd be able to get through it all somehow on a mechanical level, but it was the frustrating little things that got to me in the end. About two hours in, I was taking details of some minor traffic collision and I looked into one driver's car and I saw this cesspit, dirty ripped seats and a floor full of junk, the only clean thing in there a brand-new *Mr Submarine* sandwich box that he'd emptied and tossed into the back, and then the next thing I knew I was chasing this little fat guy down the road and he was running so hard that he obviously thought he was going to die if he stopped. That's exactly what he did, though, when a patrol car suddenly erupted out of a side-street before him and slammed to a halt blocking the way, and Travis and Leonard were out of the car holding him by the arms before I got there.

And then, when I got my breath back, I had to say, "It's okay, let him go."

"What did he do?" Travis said; and the answer was that he hadn't actually done anything. He wasn't even the culpable driver in the collision. Travis took him back to wait by his car, talking to him in a low voice, and Leonard said, "Everything all right, Alex?"

"As good as it's going to get," I said, and left them to take over.

Three blocks away I unhooked the portable radio from my dash so that I could keep in touch and went for my usual donut break, alone. This wasn't working out; Winter, and what he might have done to Georgie, were preying on my mind, but I still didn't see any way that I could act on what I'd learned. The waitress in the place knew my name, but I didn't know hers and we'd become familiar beyond the point at which I could admit it and ask; and as I was sitting by the window, she said, "Alex, can you get me some more of those Operation Identification stickers?"

There were little yellow stickers which announced that anything of value on the premises had been marked and would be traceable. I said, "What happened to the others?"

"Somebody stole them before I could put them up."

"I'll bring some more next time."

The shop was almost empty, so she came over. She

said, "You're looking tired. Did you get a vacation this year?"

"I took a trip upstate," I said. "It didn't work out."

Five minutes later, I was back in my car and heading back to base. I'd had a radio call to say that someone was waiting to see me in the station yard. Considering the goings-on of the last couple of weeks, it could have been anything; I wouldn't have been surprised to find Doctor Elaine Mulholland demanding to know why I wouldn't even phone her to explain the appointments that I kept missing. But what I found instead was an ordinary patrolman in an ordinary patrol car from the north-eastern district, sent to collect me and take me out into the desert to the marked spot found that morning by one of our helicopters.

It was the grave. It had to be. Not enough time had passed for traces to be covered over completely, and the disturbance of the ground would be even more apparent from the air. I now had the length of one car ride to come up with the explanation that I'd so far avoided even considering.

Nothing promising seemed to be offering itself.

But as we came out of the yard and along by the airport, the patrolman was saying, "It looked like a grave, but the lab people spent the last three hours taking the dirt out with little spoons and they didn't find a thing."

"It was empty?" I said.

"It had been dug over, but nothing was there. The reason you haven't heard is that they've been keeping it off the radio so that the press people won't get to hear about it and come trampling around. Listen, can you read the map for me when we get closer? I'm not a hundred per cent sure of the turnoff."

"Of course," I said, and found the folded city map in the door pocket beside me. I left it open on my knees, even though I wouldn't need it when we got there. I knew the turnoff only too well.

So the grave was empty. Only Winter could have done it, because only Winter and I had known where it was; and of the two of us, probably only Winter had the long-time familiarity with the desert to be able to find the exact spot again. What was the point? I wondered. There had to be one, and I somehow didn't think that it would turn out to be anything that I'd like.

We headed out into the desert by the old broken stake. The dirt road didn't look any more heavily-used than it had last time, but then the earth was probably baked as hard as concrete. The patrolman said, "Your liaison guy, Michaels. Is he all right?"

"Most of the time," I said, thinking that most of the time didn't include the hours since he'd walked out of the so-called 'massacre house'. The patrolman nervously changed his grip on the wheel, and I could see that he had a delicate point to make.

He said, "Well, maybe you could have a word with him. He's wandering around like he hardly knows what he's doing. He walked off into the desert this morning and didn't reappear for almost an hour." And then he glanced over at me with a brief, apologetic smile, and I realised then that this was the real, if unofficial, reason for me being summoned along, not because there was some new dimension to the Paradise connection but because Michaels was on the slide and needed someone to quietly take him home. Business had to continue, and the massacre house hero was becoming an embarrassment.

There were only a couple of cars and a van remaining when we got there, first glimpsed through the heat haze but firming-up as we got closer. The lab people had taken their samples and covered the grave site with polythene sheet, staking it down against the possibility of wind and adding stones for extra certainty. Now they were stowing their gear away, their hair in sweat-spikes and their shirts patched dark.

Twenty minutes later, they and the patrolman had gone. They left me, and Michaels, and Michaels' car.

He hadn't said more than two words to me in all of that time, one of which had been *Hi* and the other of which had been *Alex*. He'd spent most of it carefully treading the dust around the edge of the site, arms folded and his eyes on the ground in front of him as if looking for lost money. I'd seen the lab people exchanging glances about him as if having him around made them uncomfortable – which is pretty

122

rich, if you know lab people at all. But in this case, I couldn't blame them.

Watching as the dirt-clouds raised by the departing vehicles slowly dispersed towards the horizon, I wondered how I was going to open this conversation. Time seemed to take a beat.

But then, Michaels was the one who spoke first.

He said, "Let's not kid each other, Alex, okay?"

I turned to him. The peak of his uniform cap shaded his eyes, somehow making his gaze seem all the more intense. It was like talking to somebody wearing mirror sunglasses, which I've never liked to do.

I said, "Kid each other about what?"

"I was at the Paradise when it started. I've seen the sequence, too."

I said warily, "What sequence is this?"

"Don't make me put it into words, Alex. I don't want to hear myself saying those things. I've been walking around these last two days and it's like I've been able to feel my mind slipping away, one piece at a time. But then I put you and that business with Woods into the picture, and it all came together again."

"I mistook the guy, that's all," I persisted, and he stared at me for a few moments longer. I couldn't even guess what he might be thinking.

Then he said, "Come with me."

He turned and set off into the desert without looking back. I hesitated a moment, then started to follow. I didn't know if he'd fastened on the truth, or what. He might even have reached something like the right conclusion, but for all the wrong reasons; the only safe course was to watch, and let him speak, and give away as little as possible.

But life had turned pretty interesting again in the last couple of minutes.

I glanced back at the car several times, uneasy at the chance of losing sight of it. We seemed to be covering quite a distance, and a light breeze would have been enough to wipe away our tracks in the dust and leave us stranded; but the air was still and hot, and furthermore Michaels seemed to have a definite sense of where he was going.

"I saw birds overhead," he said at last. "That's what led me here."

We'd reached the side of a shallow canyon, a straight-sided cleft that had been cut by some long-vanished river. It went down about fifteen feet, no more, and the scrubby growth of the desert had intensified and become almost lush in its shelter. Michaels scrambled down the side, and began to make his way along the canyon floor; I followed in his wake, feeling absurdly like a kid on a dare.

Where the canyon turned about fifty yards further on, one of the sides formed a shady overhang and it was here that I got my first glimpse of our destination. A bleached adobe wall showed through the prickly bushes, its edges crumbling away, and I could see other shapes and structures in the unmistakable pattern of a ruined pueblo built into the canyon side. How long it had stood there, I couldn't have said; some of these things go back a thousand years or more.

This one hadn't been so big, only about seven or eight windowless rooms, and most of these were now open to the sky. We went in through what had once been a doorway, and climbed a step into the next chamber. This was the biggest of the complex, and looked to be the most complete. Michaels stepped aside to let me pass.

Before me, on an earthen dais that had once served some other purpose but which now had the look of nothing less than a primitive throne, sat the body of Woods. Someone had taken a lot of trouble with it. He was crusted with desert dirt and his time in the dry ground had sucked all of the moisture from his flesh, stretching his skin tight and drawing his lips back in a tight oval. It gave him the look of those Vietcong dead in the newsreels. His arms were spread wide and had been converted to form crude wings by the addition of twigs, brush, feathers, and scraps of cloth; and in the hollow that had been his skull, a rounded boulder sat neatly like an egg in a cup. However he'd come to be here, it was pretty certain that he hadn't walked.

It was another joke, of course. I didn't have to see a caption to know that it would read something like *Phoenix in Flight*. I could see that his eyes were gone, probably pecked out like a lamb's.

Michaels said, "*Now* have you got anything to tell me?"

Woods may not have had many friends in life, but in death he'd found plenty of admirers, all of them flies. I turned away. I said, "How come you kept this to yourself?"

"Because I wanted *you* to see it," Michaels said, and there was desperation in his voice. "Because if you don't open up to me, Alex, we get nowhere. My guess is that you killed him and he came back, am I right? So now I've got *your* problem because I can't tell that to the investigators. But you know better, don't you, Alex? Because you killed him, and he came back, and now all of this is just to show you that he's too powerful to be stopped."

Time to take a gamble. What did I have to lose, after all?

"He can be stopped," I said.

I saw the relief in Michaels' eyes. "So what went wrong?"

"He was lucky."

We moved through into the next chamber, away from all the insect life, leaving Woods to hold court in an empty room. I sat on the rubble of an inside wall and Michaels stayed on his feet, as if he was too hungry to rest. He already knew most of the story from being involved in it, but I filled him in on some of the scenes where he hadn't been present. Then, after the details, came the speculation.

"This is amazing," he kept saying. "This is incredible."

"Number one," I said, "he's *old*. That's the key to everything he thinks and does. You've got to think of what the worst old people can be like, and then multiply it a hundred times over. He's set in his ways, not flexible like a creature like him really needs to be. He kept going back to the same motels over and over out of habit, and that's why he was so easy to find again. He knows how to drive, but he doesn't seem to like to. And he's crabby, he hates young people . . . and to him, *everybody*'s young. I don't think he only hates youth, I think he hates life itself – he's been around too long and it's gone sour in him. But his nature won't allow him even to consider the idea of giving it up, so he takes it out on the rest of us. He knows to keep his head down for most of the time, but every now and again it comes bursting out and we get the killings and the mutilations. Right now more than ever, because I found a weakness in him and his pride's been dented."

I picked up one of the flat stones that had once been a part of the wall, and hefted it from hand to hand. Michaels shifted his weight from one foot to the other, still listening, still unable to relax.

I said, "Point number two, he's not very bright. What he can do makes him look awesome, but stop for a minute and look how he uses it. He says he's been around for ever, and where does it lead him? To the Paradise Motel in the Deuce, low-life all the way. He ought to be living like a king, but he can't handle or hang onto money. Even when I thought I'd found his weakness and wiped him out he could have slipped away and broken the trail for good, but instead he comes back screaming and pointing the finger at me like some outraged old prima donna. It occurred to me that he probably isn't the only one of his kind, but the rest of them are smart enough never to be seen. They don't rip up children and they don't make waves – they just keep on surviving and probably do pretty well. So perhaps this one's just the visible rogue of an invisible species, I don't know. What I *do* know is that essentially he's a loser, and he *can* be stopped."

"So," Michaels said, "what's our lever?"

"I've been thinking about the way he works. I mean, the way he's put together. The quickest way to release him is just to kill the body that he's in. I've seen him do it without, but it takes concentration. Give him a bang on the head or knock him unconscious, and it messes him up enough to keep him in one place for a while; that's how come he couldn't escape a beating when he was Mercado, and how I was able to hold onto him when he was Woods. The point is that he has to have another body to go to, and fast. Without that he'll just piss away into nothing."

"You sure?"

"I saw the look on his face when he thought it was coming. I'm sure of it, all right. It would have worked, too, if he hadn't got lucky in a hospital Emergency Room just a couple of blocks away. But I'll tell you something else. I don't think he realises it, but deep-down it's what he wants."

"How do you figure that?"

I turned the stone over in my hand. No Indian writing on it. "He's old, but he's not wise. He's constantly on the run. He's so jaded that he uses child-murder like other people use hard drugs. And all that he has to look forward to is a life everlasting in the Paradise Motel."

"You're saying that he actually wants to die?"

"I'm saying that he can't handle the idea, because dying's something that only happens to other people. But he waited for me on the morning after I'd made him, and he opened up when he could have walked away. He says he doesn't know why he let me get so near, but I do. I think he's chosen me. And one way or another, I intend to track him down and deliver."

"Just about what I was afraid of," Michaels said. "Sorry, Alex. You got closer than anybody." And he drew his revolver and fired at me with a sudden blast that shook the canyon.

He was faster than I'd been expecting, but he obviously wasn't used to the weight of the gun and the shot went wide by a couple of feet. I threw the rock as hard as I could, slamming in just under the breastbone. His reaction was way out of proportion to the severity of the blow, and I knew then that I'd made a right guess; I didn't wait around to watch the after-effects, but rolled back over and into the shelter of the low wall as he folded. I didn't want to stay around and give him a second try at me.

I scrambled along in the shelter of the wall, getting right out of the pueblo and into the canyon before he could recover. He came out shooting, but I could tell from the sound that he didn't know which way I'd gone. By then I was safely into a crack in the canyon wall, and could even risk a look out through the bushes without being seen; he'd wasted three shots, and was standing by the ruined doorway with his free hand clutching at his stomach as if he was afraid that it might split and let everything come spilling out.

Obviously, his belly was still bruised and sore from the killer-blow that had stopped Michaels' heart; I didn't see how else the body of a child could have accomplished it. He must have been waiting inside that small receptacle within the massacre house for the first policeman to come along, ready to cry out and draw him in alone; and then, what better guise than that of total innocence to get close enough to deliver the death-stroke? Michaels hadn't had a chance, he'd walked straight into it. His lack of concentration, his inattention to the job over the last couple of days – they weren't symptoms of an emotional reaction, they were his cover for the fact that he didn't know what he was supposed to be doing for most of the time. And all to one purpose – to find out how vulnerable he really was, to find out how much I knew.

And I'd told him now, hadn't I?

As long as he was in Michaels' body, he should have given himself some practice with Michaels' gun; if he'd been a little more expert, then I'd have been dessert for the pueblo flies. But like I'd told him, in some ways he obviously wasn't too bright.

Now he was walking away from me, scanning the canyon floor for signs of where I might have gone. He wasn't bothering to keep to cover. I was a better shot than him, and could have put four into his back before he hit the ground . . . but where would it have got me, in the long run?

And there were some things I wanted to know.

Almost at the turn of the canyon, he seemed to give up and look all around him.

"Alex," he called out, "this is silly. Can't we talk?"

His voice, raised as it was, echoed from the canyon sides and came back at me from three different directions at once. Would the trick work both ways? I decided to give it a try. I could always drop him, if he zeroed in on me. After coming so far, there was no point in worrying about adding to his annoyance. I'd simply increase my own personal body count and the chances of a final reckoning, that was all.

So I called back, "I thought that was what we were doing."

It seemed to work. His head swung around, but he hadn't placed me. It was strange to watch. This was the first time I'd seen him as someone that I already knew. It wasn't as if Michaels had died; but it certainly wasn't as if he lived, either.

He said, "So I flew off the handle. Is that so surprising, after some of the things you said? Come on out."

"I'm fine here."

"It's your chance to ask me about the child."

Ah.

There was his hold over me, and he knew it. I said, "What about her?"

"She's safe. I haven't done a thing to her. Can you believe that?"

"I can believe anything." I didn't believe him. "But what's the catch?"

I saw him grin. He was talking to the wall; I don't know if he was aiming towards some point where he imagined me to be, or what. He said, "No catch, just a deal. You leave me alone, I'll leave her alone. How does that sound?"

"Sounds as if . . ." I began, and was immediately drowned out as he brought up the gun and fired three rocketingly loud shots into a bush that was at least a good fifty feet away from me.

I paused for the echoes to die down, and then went on, "Sounds as if you don't plan to let her go."

He was unfazed by his failure. "Come on," he said. "Put yourself in my position. Would you?"

I thought it over. Georgie alive and unhurt was about the only thing in the world that could be guaranteed to keep me at bay. Could I credit him with enough intelligence to have realised the fact all by himself? I supposed that I'd have to. After all, overplaying his lack of mental agility could be even more dangerous than failing to perceive it in the first place.

I said, "So, where are my guarantees?"

"Oh," he said, "don't worry, I don't expect you to trust me. I'll phone you at your house tomorrow, before you go out on your shift. I'll let you talk to her. You can ask her one question, something that I couldn't know, and that's *all* you ask her because I'll be listening. No traps or traces, Alex, or she'll suffer. Can we agree on that?"

I took a deep breath before replying. "Yes," I said.

"Good." He sounded as if he was pleased with the conclusion of a neat piece of business. He returned the gun to its holster, dusted off his hands, and straightened his shirt. Then, passing close by my hiding place – I didn't breathe or move – he walked back to the rough scramble-slope by which we'd first entered the canyon.

At the top, he paused and looked back; the sky behind him was almost too bright to look at. A few loose stones were still sliding down as he said, "By the way. The child stays safe, but the show goes on. Enjoy it, Alex. It's your benefit performance."

When I got to the rim and cautiously put my head up, I was half-expecting to find him waiting; but he was already most of the way back to his car, a tiny figure on that vast plain. There was something in the way that he was walking that I now recognised, as if he was no longer bothering to disguise it. What I saw was Woods' walk, cocky and self-assured and probably pre-dating Woods by some consider-able time.

In his place, I'd have stayed around a while longer and made the most of my advantage. But it occurred to me then, thinking over that parting shot about a 'benefit performance', that I was really the only audience that he had. As long as Georgie lived, my hands would be tied . . . and I'd be able to do nothing other than watch his parade of terror as he made the most of the spotlight after living in darkness.

And I still knew enough to be a threat to him, in the end. So in his eyes, the show could only have one logical final act. We'd bargained and he'd deferred it for a while, that was all.

It was only when I saw the plume of dust that marked his car's exit from the desert that I emerged all the way out of the canyon.

I had some walking to do.

PART THREE

Life in Darkness

20

I suppose that I ought to have waited at least until the sun had dropped behind the mountains, but I didn't. I was remembering the way that Woods had struck out from the dirt road on foot with such confidence, his long experience obviously telling him the shortest way back, and I was planning to take the same line. Then, if the darkness should fall, I'd at least have the sky-glow of the city to follow. I've never been able to get the hang of this business of navigating by the stars. Every direction always looks the same to me.

I'd done worse. I'd done this kind of thing at double-time and with a full pack; the trick was in taking it steady and staying cool on the inside. Within ten minutes I was back at the grave-site, picturing what I'd seen through the scope lens and looking for a piece of horizon that matched the background. At a guess, Woods had been striking out towards the Beeline Highway when my rifle bullet had rearranged his hairstyle.

In less than an hour I came to a small road that saw more regular use, a fact betrayed by the bundles of tumbled rags and mincemeat that were the leftovers of last night's roadrunners. I was doing fine, but dehydration was starting to make me feel lightheaded. I followed the road south, and another half-hour brought me the sounds of the distant highway; but before that, only a quarter of a mile ahead, I could see a half-finished white adobe structure with a couple of trucks outside it. A big sign on the front said that the building was going to be an Indian craft center when it opened sometime next year, but I didn't plan to wait. I walked in and said hi, and nearly frightened the crap out of a big long-haired guy up a ladder.

It was unbelievably cool and dark inside those three-foot walls, or at least it seemed that way to me. There were five of them working, all Indians and curious to know how a scruffy and sweat-stained cop came to be strolling in out of the desert haze. I told them some story about how the electrics on my patrol car had died and taken the radio out, so it had been walk or else just sit around hoping that someone might miss me. They had a standpipe for water but it wasn't fit for drinking, so they gave me some sweet juice from their coolbox and then one of them drove me back to Sky Harbor in the smaller of the two trucks. He dropped me in the yard, and I went into the locker room through the side-door so nobody would see the state I was in; once inside I stripped off and got straight into the shower. About half of it got onto me, the rest I think I drank.

These immediate problems had been keeping my mind off my longer-term troubles, but now these were starting to reassert themselves. It all came down to one simple fact; that if he truly had Georgie and she was still alive, not just another of his inert puppets, then my hands were tied. He had absolute leverage, and I had nothing.

The shift wasn't over, but I knew that my duties had been covered and I didn't feel in much of a fit state to go out again; the same was doubly true of my uniform, and my spare wasn't at the station. Everything considered, I was persuaded that I ought to keep my head down and go home. The skin on my forearms and in the V just under my collarbone was starting to itch and burn, and I wanted to get some Solarcaine onto it.

Having sneaked out of the station, I was then faced with the prospect of sneaking back into my own house because one or both of Loretta's in-laws were moving around in the kitchen of the house next door. I sat out in the car for a while. I handled awkward situations every day in my job, so why was I so reluctant to face up to this one? Because it was so close to home, I supposed.

I got out of the car and climbed the wooden steps to Loretta's door.

It was the man, Heilbron, who answered. "Yes?" he said, and he somehow seemed eager and distracted at the same time. He was probably somewhere in his sixties, well-worn and friendly-looking and not made for misery.

He also looked as if he'd lost weight some time over the last couple of years, and he hadn't yet grown used to it.

I said, "I'm sorry if I'm disturbing you. I live next door. I was wondering how Loretta was coming along."

"Would you be Alex?"

"That's me. Is she talking again, now?"

"On and off. Can I ask you to come in for a minute, Alex? There's so much we don't understand, here."

He stepped aside to allow me in, and I knew that I couldn't refuse. "I don't know that I can throw much light," I said, but he gestured towards the inside. It was an invitation, not a demand.

"Please," he said, so I went on through.

They'd got the place a lot neater than Loretta had ever been able to manage, but it was a dead and unlived-in kind of neatness that wasn't exactly pleasing to see. The only mess was over on the table, where a heap of Georgie's schoolbooks and drawing-pads had been stacked up for careful examination as if by a valuer. Their son's photograph, I noticed, had been brought out of the bedroom and put in a more prominent place over by the stereo.

Heilbron waved me towards a chair, and started opening cupboard doors. I was remembering the lies that I'd told to Loretta in the hospital – white lies, I'd considered them then – and was wondering if they were going to return to accuse me now.

"They say you were actually with her," he said, rummaging and not finding what he was looking for. I stood by the chair, unable to bring myself to sit. He seemed to be alone in the house.

"Not when it happened," I said, "but up to a couple of hours before."

"So you're as much in the dark as the rest of us?"

"I don't know where Georgie is," I said. "If I did, I wouldn't be wasting time around here."

He muttered something, moved on to the next cupboard. "I've been waiting here in case the phone should ring," he said. "If there's any kind of news, I don't want to miss it. Clara's staying at the hospital for most of the time."

"What are the doctors saying now?"

"Her neck was broken, but the spinal cord's still in one

135

piece so they don't think she's going to be paralysed. I can't believe how lucky she's been. They say that if somebody untrained had tried to pull her out of the wreck, that would have been the end of it. The main danger now is this haemorrhage business."

I said, fishing cautiously, "Have they got any ideas at all about Georgie?"

He gave up on the cupboards, and started on the drawers. "Not one," he said. "As many theories as you like, but nothing solid. I mean, if somebody's kidnapped her for ransom or something like that, I don't know what I'm going to do . . . I'm retired, I'm not worth much." With a sudden, impatient gesture, he slammed shut the drawer that he'd been looking through. "Damn it, Alex," he said.

"What's wrong?"

He turned to me, obviously out at the end of his line.

He said, "Have you *any* idea where Loretta keeps her booze?"

I took him through into the kitchen, and showed him the cardboard box with the bottles in it that she kept behind the spin-dryer. I could see that he desperately wanted to talk to somebody, and I felt guilty because I knew that I couldn't give him the information that would reassure him. He'd want to take it to the police, the police would treat it as a normal kidnap, and Woods, Winter, or whatever he was calling himself now, would simply kill Georgie and change his face and move on.

He rinsed out a couple of glasses at the sink, and we took a half-full bottle of scotch over to the table where the schoolbooks were. We sat, he poured.

He said, "I gather the two of you are fairly close."

"It was moving that way," I said cautiously, uncomfortably aware of the framed picture behind me.

Heilbron said, "You're not going to hurt my feelings if you say yes. We're all grown-ups here."

"I know," I said.

"We think of her like our own daughter. I only wish we could see her more, but . . . you can't stifle kids. You can't live on top of them, looking over their shoulder all the time. You understand me?"

"I certainly do."

"But then, of course, it means we don't see Georgie so often . . . and kids of that age, you blink and they've got bigger . . . where *is* she, Alex? Who took her?"

I picked up one of the schoolbooks and turned it over in my hands. "Hard to say," I said.

"I drove out to where it happened. Went over every inch and looked in every culvert, just in case she might have been thrown out and could still be lying there. I don't understand it. I don't understand a single thing about it."

He topped-up our glasses, and I explained the department's missing-persons procedure and the extra measures that we took whenever a child was involved. I was only half-listening to myself, knowing that I was covering up, but Heilbron was taking it all in like a starving dog with its eyes on a handful of biscuits. I could feel the truth like a bubble inside me, trembling and threatening to burst, and I had to leave my glass untouched because already I could feel the booze etching away at the edges of my will. It would be so easy to let go and tell. But they say that it's the same kind of thing with drowning.

Loretta, I learned, now remembered nothing of the accident or of our conversation in the hospital recovery room, probably as a result of the post-operative trauma involved in her second bout of emergency treatment. I also learned a lot about the insurance business, which was the field that Heilbron had worked in before he'd retired.

Finally I said, "I'm going to have to go."

"I know," Heilbron said, "I'm sorry. I've been talking too much."

"No, it isn't that."

"I've appreciated you being here. I want you to know something, Alex."

I pushed away the drawing book that I'd been leafing through, filled with colored-in pictures of animals and birds, and said, "What?"

"You're not the dull person you seem to think you are. You're reliable, but that's something completely different. I want you to think about that."

"I will," I promised.

"You sure you won't have one more drink with me?"

"I'd really like to," I said, standing and pushing the chair back. "But I have to take an important call in the morning."

If only you knew, I thought as I crossed the narrow patch of ground to my own place.

21

I was up at dawn the next morning. I didn't dare dress, or go in the shower, or do anything that would prevent me from getting to the phone within the first couple of rings. I walked around in a bathrobe and couldn't even sit for more than a couple of minutes at a time. Today I was on Second Watch, which meant a mid-afternoon start, so I could stick around for as long as I needed to. Somehow it never occurred to me that he wouldn't call.

He did, on the dot of eleven.

All that tension, and now I hesitated before I picked it up. But then I snatched the receiver from the cradle and said, "Yes?"

"Hello, Alex."

It was a voice that I'd heard once before, on the line at the motel up in red rock country when I'd been told that I wasn't so hard to find. I said, "Is that you, Winter?"

"Damned if I can remember," the voice said pleasantly. "Is Winter the college kid?"

"Yes."

"Then that's who I am today. His eyes aren't so good, but he's fitter than most. I've used some real wrecks to get by, in my time."

"You said I could speak to Georgie."

He made a sound of disappointment, of disapproval, but I could tell that he was playing with me. "Little hasty today, aren't we, Alex?" he said.

"Are you going to put her on, or not?"

"She's right here. Remember, Alex, one question and nothing more."

I could hear fumbling around at the other end of the line, and some whispering. I couldn't make out what was being said, but I thought that I heard my own name in there somewhere. After what seemed like forever, I heard her voice.

"Hello?" she said.

I wasn't going to allow myself to get carried away. Not yet. I said, "It's me, Georgie. I can't talk for long, but I'm going to ask you something and it's important. It may not seem so but believe me, it is."

"Okay."

"You remember your history book from school? No, don't answer that, just think about it. Somebody wrote his name on your history book and you tried to rub it off, but it wouldn't come. If you turn it to the light, you can still read it. Whose name is that, Georgie?

"On my history book?" She was taking the question seriously, at least, and not messing around and making perplexed noises like an adult might.

"On the back," I said.

"That was David Haber. He's awful, and he won't leave me alone."

I sat down heavily, because relief had made my legs go shaky. She was safe, she was whole. There was no way that Winter could have known the answer – I hadn't even known about the book myself, until I'd seen it last night – and so I knew now that he wasn't speaking through her to fool me.

I said, "That's fine. I can't talk any more right now, Georgie. Put your friend back on, will you?"

"Okay," she said, and then there was more fumbling around. She'd sounded fine; a little on-guard and apprehensive, perhaps, but not as if she was being kept in fear. I wished that I could see what was happening there at the other end of the line, get some idea of exactly how and where she was being held.

When Winter came back on, he said in a voice of exasperation, "Jesus, Alex!"

I said, "What's the matter?"

"I give you one simple question to ask and you have to make a whole production out of it. Are you satisfied now?"

"Depends what you call satisfied."

"Oh, don't play games. Do you believe she was speaking for herself?"

"Yes," I said.

"Good. Now leave me alone, and that's how she stays. She's safe, she's being looked after, she's got everything she needs."

"And how long are we supposed to be able to go on like this?"

"For however long I say we do," he shot back, and I could hear the iron of arrogance lying just underneath his words. "You're not in control here, Alex, *I* am. Be by that phone every day at this time. I may call, I may not, but when I *do*, you'd better be there. Anytime you're not, that finishes it."

"What if there's trouble with the phone?"

"Then it's bad luck for both of you. The child's here with me, so I don't think you'll want me to say what happens then. But you get the picture, don't you, Alex?"

"I get the picture," I said, and he hung up on me.

I'd dented his good mood, and I wished I hadn't. I didn't want to score points off him, he could too easily take it out on Georgie. But at least I now knew that she was all right, and I'd spoken to her; she'd sounded calm, too calm if anything. If I'd worried before about her being thrust too fast into a premature kind of adulthood, I had more to be troubled about now. I didn't know what she'd been seeing or what she may have learned, but I knew that it wouldn't be the kind of knowledge that you'd get from *Sesame Street*.

I sat there by the phone a while longer, looking at my empty hands. What was I going to do?

I was going to do exactly what I'd been told.

When I went out a couple of hours later, I had my spare uniform on a hanger for wearing and the other one in a plastic sack for the laundry. As I was putting them both into the back of my car, Heilbron was getting something out of his. He squinted at me, a non desert-dweller unused to the sunlight, and said, "Hello again, Alex. The phone didn't ring while I was out, did it?"

"I don't believe so."

"Only, I had a brainwave. Picked up this." He brought it over to show me; it turned out to be a telephone answering machine in a box. "Eighty-five dollars but the man said it works like new. Now if somebody calls and I have to be out, I won't have to worry about whether I missed it."

"Good idea," I said.

"I don't suppose you know anything about fixing them up?"

"Not a thing."

"Well," he said, turning the box over and looking all around it as if for clues, "I ought to be able to manage. There's supposed to be a booklet somewhere in here." And then he turned kind of sheepish and serious. "Listen, Alex . . ."

"What?"

"I'm sorry if I rambled last night. I'll bet you thought I was never going to shut up."

"Didn't even cross my mind," I said.

"Well . . . thanks for coming around, anyway. It did me good."

And me as well, I supposed. I said, "Any time. Except now. Now I have to work."

He didn't take offence, as I'd known that he wouldn't. He said, "Listen, if you should hear anything at all . . ."

"I'll find you," I promised.

He walked to the site entrance and waved me off down the road. It was years since anybody had done anything remotely like that for me. But then I suppose that I'd lost a father, and he'd lost a son . . . we were like pieces from two different puzzles, we may not have matched but we more or less fit. I liked him, he was all right.

But now it was back to business.

Michaels, I learned at the station, had phoned in sick. This was to everybody's relief and to nobody's surprise except mine; I couldn't understand why he'd bothered. Within ten minutes of being on the road almost the entire Watch was involved in a major scramble when we had a call from somewhere on North 40th Street for a domestic quarrel with shots heard; the address turned out to be somewhere in a labyrinthine estate whose roads followed no comprehensible system and which had no less than ten units screeching around and almost shunting one another as they crossed at the intersections. The cause of the panic proved in the end to be an over-loud TV set. After that there was a kind of lull in the action, and I took advantage of the quiet period to slip out of the area and drive out towards the quiet street where Michaels had lived.

I'd been there once before, but that had been before his wife had taken a college place somewhere back east to begin belated work on her Master's degree. I didn't know what kind of arrangement they had now. The place seemed dead and silent as I walked up the short path to the door, anyway; I rang the bell, but nobody came.

It was a one-story house, no more than three or four years old, with close neighbors but a well-screened boundary of masonry walls and bushes between each property. It wasn't bad, not bad at all. I knew that Michaels topped up his salary with all kinds of business interests; in fact he'd once told me that he looked upon policework more as a recreation and a labor of love than as a career, to the extent that he'd declined to take the captains' exam because he didn't want to be taken off the streets.

Well, he was off them now.

I went around to the back, through a gate which should have been bolted but which wasn't, into a yard where a stepped redwood deck overlooked a small swimming pool. There were leaves on the surface of the pool, and the patio door beyond stood open a couple of feet.

I unclipped my holster. Just in case.

The whole house had been pretty thoroughly turned-over. Drawers had been turned out and dumped, clothes pulled out of the closets and strewn, pictures clawed down from the walls in the search for a concealed safe. He'd uncovered one in the study, an iron safe with a combination lock, and although it was scratched and chipped he hadn't been able to get it open. Michaels' certificates of business practise still hung on the wall to either side. The desk beneath had been plundered and things like files and deeds and ranch prospectuses had been thrown around in the hunt for cash and petty valuables to pawn. It was low, it was petty, it made me sick. To be able to live forever, and to choose to live like this.

I noticed one other thing before I left, and that was a letter lying on the mat behind the door. It had yesterday's postmark, and must have been delivered this morning. I didn't have to open it to know what was inside, because I recognised the stationery of Doctor Elaine Mulholland. Poor old Doc, sitting there in an empty office and none of her patients putting in an appearance. I hoped it wouldn't give her a complex, or anything.

Five minutes later I was back in my own area and responding to a call. No-one had even noticed that I'd been gone.

22

It was two whole days before he called me again, days that seemed to drag on forever. The city was quiet, although the fear was still everywhere; the sale in guard dogs was so heavy that animals were having to be trucked in from out of state, and gun shops couldn't keep up with the demand. One of the local radio stations took to playing *Psycho Killer* by Talking Heads until their board of management told them to stop, after which phone-in requests for the track increased tenfold. I read in the *Phoenix Gazette* that a small-time movie producer had taken a suite in the Hyatt and announced that he was going to step in and bid for the killer's story, as soon as he was caught. According to the paper his last movie had been *Revenge of the Killer Zombies* and I sat there in the coffee shop, giggling and snorting helplessly and thinking Christ, if only he *knew*. Out on the streets, we had to cope with local vigilante groups who organised their own patrols and generally got in the way. We even had to break up a fight between two of them.

I was expecting him to hit again, and he probably knew it and was drawing me out as far as he could; but at least that way, nobody was dying.

Nobody that we were hearing about, anyway.

The next time he called, I had Winter's photograph – the one that I'd taken from his room – propped on the table by the phone. After making me wait for so long, at least he was punctual about the hour. I picked up the phone after two rings, and heard Winter's voice say, "Me again."

"Still sticking with the college boy, huh?"

"He's clean, no sign of any bad habits. But I only keep him for around the house, so don't go expecting to see him on the streets. I've got other faces for that."

Winter looked back at me out of the photograph. A plain, ordinary, smiling kid. But only an instrument, now.

I said, "How many faces do you have?"

"You really want to waste today's question on me?"

"I take it back."

"That's better. Here's Georgina."

He seemed to be in a playful mood today. And why not? He had everything under control, after all. I heard the phone being passed over, and Georgie came on the line and said, "Hi, Alex."

"Hello, Georgie," I said. "You know the rules we have to play by?"

"You get to ask me a question, and I have to answer it."

Winter must have been right there with his ear up against the receiver, because without a break he cut in and said, "Was that it? Not very illuminating, I must say," and put the phone down on me.

I sat there clutching the buzzing phone in disbelief, but it was already too late. I cradled it and paced the room in impotent fury, running my fingers through my hair and unable to decide what to do next.

But then the phone rang again, and I dashed over and snatched it up.

"Admit it," Winter said happily, "I had you worried."

"Stop playing around," I said. "Put her back on."

I could hear him laughing in the background as he handed over again. Georgie came on and said, "He didn't mean that. He was only joking."

"Yeah," I said, "he's a real comedian. Answer me this, Georgie. Are you scared?"

She thought about it for a moment. "I was at first," she said, "but not so much now that he's explained some things to me. I've got my own room and a TV, and he brings me comic books and stuff. I asked for a bird in a cage, and he says he'll get me one. It's not like jail, or anything."

"Does he lock you in?"

"Of course I lock her in," Winter said unexpectedly, because this time the changeover at the far end had been quick and silent, "but she understands why it has to be done. I wish I could say as much for you."

"I got what I wanted."

"You mean that was it? No catch-me-out question, just a welfare enquiry? Alex, does this mean you're beginning to *trust* me?"

"I'd trust Nixon before I'd trust you," I said. "I genuinely wanted to know." And now that I knew, I liked the situation even less, impossible as that seemed. I didn't like the rapport that he and Georgie seemed to be building up – something entirely manufactured from his end, I didn't doubt, but Georgie couldn't see through that. I felt very much like the outsider butting in, here.

Winter said, "Don't worry about her, Alex, she's getting everything she could possibly want. You think I don't know how to spoil a child?"

"Don't tempt me," I said.

There was a moment's silence while I waited for his reaction, and then: "A joke! You know, Alex, you may not believe this, but I've been getting to like you."

"Just what I always wanted."

"Poor, dull, unimaginative Alex. Thrust right into the middle of something that he can hardly believe, and he can't breathe a word about it to anybody because they won't believe him either. I feel for you, I really do."

I said, "If you like me so much, will you listen to a suggestion?"

"It costs me nothing to listen," he said.

I wasn't looking at the photograph of Winter now, I was looking at the face that had formed in my mind; it was composite, ugly, a kind of soft clay that could boil and mutate but which retained the essence of evil in any shape that it took. Being on the phone made it easier to visualise; and visualising made it easier to say what I had to say next.

"Meet me one-to-one," I said. "You can be whoever you like as long as you wipe out all the reserves first. I'll meet you on equal terms and we'll see who walks away."

He seemed amused by the proposal. "What makes you think I'd agree to something like that?"

"Because you've already thought of it. Every time we meet up, you've got an escape hatch – which means that every time, it ends with you running away. But I'll bet you've wondered, what would happen if we both had to see it through to the finish?"

"You'd lose," he said flatly. But was there just a small hint of uncertainty in there?

"Easy enough to say," I persisted. "Admit it, you're scared of me a little."

"Scared of you? Why?"

"Because unless you've got me pinned down like you have now, you don't know where I'll be coming from next. And I think that's why you say you like me, as well, why you don't just break the chain and move on to some other town. I've put some spice into your life, and you'd forgotten what it can be like."

I heard him sigh. "You're an entertainment, Alex, I'll give you that," he said. "Listen, I'm going to do something for you. I can promise you something good this afternoon, and I'll try to make sure it's within your squad area. Watch for it, okay? This one's just for you."

And with that friendly promise, he ended the call.

23

After the first hour or so of the shift, I could feel the resentment stirring in my patrols and knew that I'd have to ease off on them. I was riding them too hard, and I was doing nothing to enhance their operating efficiency.

But then I knew that something was coming, whilst for them it was just a normal Watch.

I forced myself to back off, to try to function as normal even though my heart was thumping and I had this sick feeling down in my gut for most of the time. When it happened, whatever it was going to be, I knew that I'd respond and be able to function perfectly well; what tore me up was the uncertainty, like standing in the dark and waiting for some unknown hand to fall on your shoulder.

I cruised my area, staying close to my men and trying to manage at least a drive-past and visual check on every call. Mostly they'd raise a hand with the fingers extended meaning ten-four, everything's okay and no help needed. Driving around, I saw that there was some new spraycan graffiti around the Deuce; some of the gangs had picked up on the *Young Life, Old Scores* slogan and I noticed it several times both in English and Spanish. Coming out onto Van Buren I was flagged down by a heavy-looking Hispanic guy who seemed to want me to know all about his wife, who was about to have a baby; and I realised why he was telling me when I turned around and saw that two of his relatives were already helping the groaning woman into the back of my car, and it was too late to do anything about it.

I looked over at his own car, which he'd pulled into the side and which seemed to contain an impossibly solid mass of people, heads everywhere and too many to count, and I said, "Okay, follow me to the hospital. Don't try to keep up with me, and don't cross any red lights."

The woman herself spoke no English, but her two sisters had stayed with her and were able to translate. I mainly wanted to tell her not to mess up my seat, but what I said was, "Ask her if the pains are continuous, or if they're like every minute or so."

There was a quick gabble in the back, and then one of the sisters said, "She says it's both."

"Well, then," I said confidently. 'Tell her she's got plenty of time."

The truth of it was that I had no idea, but the trick is always to make them think that you have.

We went storming up 24th Street with all the lights flashing and the siren howling to scatter the traffic, and only a few minutes later they were loading her into a wheelchair outside the County General. This was the same parking lot where I'd tried to flatten the enemy in the shape of Woods, what seemed like about three centuries ago. The husband's car arrived shortly after, and disgorged what appeared to be three complete generations of two separate families. I was checking the state of my back seat at the time, and that's how I was when I heard the call.

It was a 921, a prowler seen trying to enter an occupied apartment on the east side of the Deuce. Something in me seemed to click, and the motors began to whirr; prowlers generally only become housebreakers when they come upon a place that they know is empty. Travis and Leonard were taking the call, and I jumped in behind the wheel with the intention of racing to join them.

I must have cut through the late-afternoon traffic like a scythe. The address given was a run-down five-story block with its ground-floor windows boarded and a rusty strap-iron fire escape climbing up its side; behind it were warehouses, and beyond them the railyards. I pulled in behind the patrol vehicle and went inside. Every tenant in the block seemed to be out on the stairs swapping opinions, and I almost had to fight my way through to the third floor.

Travis was listening to a beefy man in a singlet, nodding as he listened. Leonard had climbed out through the window to take a look down the iron stairway. Even at first glance I could see that there were a few spots of blood on the sill. I asked Travis for the story.

"Kid comes into his bedroom and sees this deadbeat trying to climb in off the fire escape. The guy's got his leg through and he's struggling, so the kid pulls a shiv and starts spiking him in the thigh. That shifted him out fast enough."

I took a look around. I wouldn't have guessed that this could be a child's bedroom; there were no posters, no toys, nothing much at all other than three folding cots shoved over against the wall. I said, "How old is the kid?"

"Nine," Travis said, "and he wants to know if he's going to get a reward. That's the knife, over there."

It was lying on one of the beds, and we went over to take a look. As far as I could see it was a steel letter-opener that had been honed to a deadly point. So I'd been wrong about the total absence of toys, after all.

I said, "Any description?"

And Travis said, "Well, I guess you could start with a limp."

Leonard came up at the window then. "Sergeant?" he said, peering through the opening at me. "I think we're dealing with something more than a daytime burglar here."

"What do you mean?"

He glanced over my shoulder at the man in the singlet, who was hanging around to see what he could overhear, and said, "Come outside, and I'll show you."

We went out through the window of the next room to avoid disturbing any marks or prints on the bedroom sill, and followed Leonard down two creaking flights in the open air. Something had lodged there, something that had perhaps been dropped and had fallen through the open ironwork of the treads. We crouched down to look at it, not touching, and Travis said, "What kind of a knife is that?"

"It's a flensing knife," Leonard said. Most of the rest of his family were in the meat trade, so I supposed he ought to know. "They use them in slaughterhouses to strip the skins off carcasses."

A little shudder ran through both Travis and me then as the implications suggested themselves to us, but we didn't get long to speculate because there was another call coming through on the portable radio relay that Travis had clipped to his belt when leaving the patrol car. It was clashing with my own, a weird effect that made it seem as if the dispatcher's voice was coming from the air all around us.

"I'll give you good odds that's for the same guy," I said. "Come on." And then, in what was a deliberate lapse of professionalism, I took Travis and Leonard down with me to the cars leaving the witnesses and the physical evidence unattended; but the call was for only a couple of blocks away, and we were probably closer than anybody, and the priority now was to grab our would-be perpetrator before he could do any actual damage.

I didn't have any doubts about who we'd be looking for. The only uncertainty was that I didn't know how I might recognise him.

At least there couldn't be any doubt about the location, because when we came around the corner there was a little barrel-shaped woman out in the middle of the street waving her arms in the air at us. We pulled in to either side of her, and I got out and said, "Did you make the call?"

"I did," she said. "Some bastard asking my kids if they wanted to go with him, and then when they said no he asked them if they wanted to die."

"What did he look like? Was he limping?"

"He'll be more than limping when my man gets hold of him. They ran off over towards the yards."

Travis and Leonard took off in pursuit with a screech of rubber then, and I said, "You mean that somebody was chasing him?"

"You bet," she said. "You see what he dropped when he ran?" And she pointed over toward the sidewalk behind her, where something bundled in a rag had been dropped on the paving and had started to come open. Leaving my car door open I went to take a look, and saw an old iron-headed hammer and about seven long spike-nails. She added, "You can't miss him, he's horrible-looking, got this long brown overcoat on. It flapped around when he ran, only he didn't run so good."

So, this was the show. He was dropping his kit as he went.

I got back into my car. Other units were coming into the area by now, and I requested the Chase frequency to organise them into a ring that would effectively seal the streets for a couple of blocks in every direction. As soon as I'd done, Travis came on with a report that they had him pinned. I told the other units to hold in case he made a break, and then sped the four hundred yards or so to the location that Travis had named.

They were outside a scrapyard, by gates in a high wooden fence behind which dead cars had been stacked in towers to be watched over by the tip of a crane. The sky above was a deep, scorched blue. The patrol car had been parked across the gateway, and about half a dozen men in

150

baseball caps and most of them carrying sticks had surrounded Travis and were all talking at once. It didn't take much to guess that the blockwatch committee had pursued their quarry this far, and that he'd disappeared into the yard itself. Travis was waving them down, asking them to speak one at a time, and they were all too excited to take any notice.

I beckoned him out, as much to rescue him as anything else.

"Call in for any extra units they can spare us," I told him, "and ask them to put the SWAT team on standby. Make sure we've got coverage on all the yard's exits." While he was making a start on that, I turned to the man who seemed to be the leader of the neighborhood posse.

I said, "When you saw him go into the yard, was he carrying a gun?"

The man shook his head. "I didn't see him carrying anything," he said.

Try again. I drew my own revolver and held it up where he could see, and cocked the hammer noisily.

I said, "Was he armed and dangerous, or not?"

"Fuck yes," the man amended hastily.

Leonard had been in to alert the yard's foreman and now its small number of employees were filing out, squeezing through the deliberately narrow gap between the patrol car and the gate. They looked bewildered and uncertain. I asked Travis if he was game to go in and take a look, and Travis unholstered the tank-stopper that he carried in place of the standard weapon and said that he was.

I knew that this was, in a sense, futile, but there were several reasons why I had to go ahead with it. Besides appearances, I had to consider that beating Winter one more time might push him a little of the way towards taking on my challenge, about which I'd been deadly serious. And although in one sense we might not be playing for real at this stage, try telling that to any victims who might have had the misfortune to get in his way. We went in with our radios off, me leading the way and Travis covering our backs against any approach, moving in silence down the first of the shaded alleys of metal and chrome.

The place where we came out was an oil-stained clearing

where half-salvaged shells stood ready for the crusher. So far we'd seen no signs of life at all, unless you counted a cat which had turned and dived off into the iron jungle at the first sight of us, but now Travis touched my arm at a sound from above. He hardly needed to; there wasn't much chance of me missing the noise of a skylight trap being thrown open, and the shrieking of a woman as she was hauled out into the air.

They were up on the high corrugated roof of the yard office, which itself stood on stilts over the breaking workshop and was reached by an external stairway. From where we were standing, it was like looking up at a high-diving board. A gaunt, bony-looking man had a grip on the shoulder of a woman's dress, and it was pulling up and showing all her underwear as he dragged her out kicking. Winter had chosen well, the guy looked like a ghoul, his long brown overcoat flapping around. The screaming and the kicking stopped as the woman got a hold on the roof ridge and clung there, and one of her shoes came off and bounced three times on the corrugated iron before sailing all the way down and bouncing again off a pile of dented hubcaps, which clattered like dropped plates. The woman was probably the office help, and had somehow been missed in the staff roundup. The ghoul shaded his eyes from the sun and peered down at us, grinning, and called out, "Hiya, officers, come for the show?" And then he clambered around and straddled the ridge as his victim hung on shivering only a couple of feet away. He was moving awkwardly, dragging one of his legs, but he didn't show the slightest fear of the height or of the delicacy of his perch.

Then he looked inside his coat, thin straggly hair lifting in a breeze that wasn't touching us down below, and pulled something out which seemed to catch on the lining; it took me a moment to recognise it as an office billspike carrying a thick wad of papers, and by then he was already starting to pull the invoices off in handfuls and letting them scatter.

Travis said in a dull, oh-shit kind of voice, "He's going to do her while we watch. The marksmen aren't even here yet."

The paper flimsies were showering down over the yard now like oversized stage snow. The ghoul gave us another encouraging grin, and threw another handful as wide as he could. The spike was almost fully exposed now, about as slender and sharp as an icepick.

I said, "Let me have your magnum," and Travis, transfixed by what was going on up above, didn't quite hear me.

"Say again?"

"That Bofors gun you carry. Let me borrow it for a minute."

Travis blinked at me, then looked again at the distance, and then handed it over. I got the impression that this was something he'd be interested to see.

I put most of the blame on Clint Eastwood. Travis and some of the other younger patrolmen had been spending their own money on these big, powerful and unforgiving guns, equipping themselves with something that, for my money, is simply too much weapon for policework. In a close-quarters situation, a magnum round is liable to go straight through its target and on to hit somebody else, instead of being contained like a shot from a .38. I've heard of people taking half a dozen hits from a .38 and still surviving. With a magnum the surgery tends to be more permanent – anything vital that gets in the way, it's gone.

I used the protruding fender of an AMC Hornet to steady my arm, my left hand cupping the butt of the pistol. You see movie stars gripping the wrist of the gun arm with their free hand but that's just bullshit, it does nothing except make for a good-looking pose. I steadied my breathing and watched the tails of the ghoul's coat as they flapped in the breeze; I'd have to allow for that, shoot a little wide and to the left, or else I'd risk drifting over and hitting the woman. If she'd stay down, as she was now, then that would reduce the danger a little. I couldn't see her doing much else, she was oblivious to everything else now apart from her grip on the roof ridge . . . but I'd decided to aim extra-wide and take no chances, just in case.

The ghoul had the spike empty now, and he showed it to us for one last time.

I fired.

The spike and the hand that was holding it simply disappeared in a splattery fuzz of red. It must have looked like an amazing piece of virtuoso marksmanship, but the truth of it was that I'd calculated for a body hit and this was nothing more than fluke. My ears were ringing and my arm felt as if I'd just punched concrete, and up on the tin roof the ghoul was clambering unsteadily to his feet. With a stuck leg and one hand blown away, surely it couldn't take much more than a shift in the wind direction to push him off-balance.

He looked at his bloody sleeve, and bowed slightly. Shock probably meant that he wouldn't be feeling anything from it yet. He called out, "Good shooting, Sergeant," in a mock-courteous kind of tone, and I wondered if he was going to call me by name, but then he said, "Now watch the bird fly," and took three tottering steps down to the roof's edge and launched himself off into nowhere. I don't think the woman even knew that he'd gone, because she didn't move. He made a graceful dive, his coat flapping behind him like a torn pair of wings, and went down headfirst behind a tall stack of flattened car bodies with a bam-splatter noise like fruit going through an aircraft engine.

I didn't hand the magnum back. I was going to have to hang onto it now until the firearms team, who have to turn out and investigate every time a shot is fired by an officer, had finished with me. The SWAT team wouldn't be needed now, but perhaps a couple of their mountaineering boys could contemplate the problem of how to get the ghoul's terrified almost-victim down to safety.

"Er, listen, Sergeant," Travis said, and I could see that he was both inspired and impressed. The fact that my actual marksmanship had deserved a near-miss at best would count for nothing now. "I don't think it's any secret in the squad that we've all been a little worried about you over the past few days."

"Is that right?" I said.

"Hey, I mean, don't read anything into it, all I'm talking about is friendly concern that you might have . . . well, we know about the strain you've been under. But what I'm saying is, I take it all back. After what I just saw, even if you started turning up for duty in a dress it would be okay by me."

"Really?"

"You bet."

"It's something I hadn't considered," I said. "But thanks for the suggestion."

24

The ghoul.

There was a name that suited him as well as any, and after the end of the shift that evening I sat in my car in the station yard for a while and tried to see if I could get it to come as a natural part of my thinking about him. But I couldn't. Whenever he came into my mind it was always either as Woods or Winter or sometimes even Mercado, human names and human faces with that other and much uglier aspect only dimly glimpsed behind.

I hoped that it wouldn't cause me to be soft on him, when the time came.

I'd been given a tough grilling by the firearms investigators and this, on top of everything else, had left me keyed-up and edgy. Instead of driving straight home from the yard I turned north, and a half-hour later I was getting out of the car at the same spot on the mountain road where I'd pulled in with Loretta and Georgie on the day of the zoo trip. I leaned against the side of the car, shivering a little in the evening chill. Now, as then, the lights of the valley were glowing before me like a scattered handful of diamond dust, a network of life that spread for miles but which was contained by the distant hills, themselves no more than a dark sketch against a dying sunset. What I hadn't told Loretta was that this was somewhere that I'd found myself on the night that Eloise passed away, a long night of driving and driving with no purpose in mind other than to fill myself with the dead feeling that comes after mile upon mile of empty road. I suppose I must have stopped lots of places, but this was the only one that I ever remembered and returned to; seeing not a city but a deep, dark bowl of stars, and knowing that unless something was going to take this memory away, then I was never going to leave.

And I'd been right. My life had been in pieces once, but instead of running away I'd fitted them together again and I was whole. I think that this, more than anything else, had kept me together over the last few weeks. I had no big theories about the ghoul, all that I knew of him was what I'd seen; he was like a night-train passing through, headlamp masked and numbers covered, emerging from darkness and heading for an unknown destination, with human lives a convenient fuel for his fires. I had no doubt that we mattered to him about as much as the day-old chicks did to the hawks in the zoo . . . but I was the one who'd refused to run and had grown because of it, whereas he was running all the time. He might consider himself to be the ultimate predator, but I believed that it was the prey, in the end, who would have the stronger hold on life.

We would come through, I told the valley of lights. It would cost, but we would come through.

The chill was starting to get through to me. I had a jacket in the car, but instead I got in and started the engine and set off for home.

I was pretty sure that I'd be getting a call the next morning, and for some strange reason I slept better that night than I had in weeks. As the hour of eleven approached I was showered and dressed and ready with the day's question, and I had the radio on so that I could keep an exact track of the time as they counted down towards the on-the-hour news.

But then with about five minutes to go, somebody came and knocked on my door.

I stayed quiet and hoped that they'd go away but the radio was my let-down, proving that somebody was home – that, and the car outside, I suppose. I heard a female voice calling, "Hello, Sergeant?" and so then I had to go over and open the door.

I looked out at her through the bug screen. She was standing out on my little porch, well-tailored, trim, and put into soft-focus by being seen through the gauze. I said, "What can I do for you?"

"I'm Angela Price from KTAR News," she said. "Can I speak to you for a minute?"

I opened the bug screen for a better look. And what do you know? It was exactly who I'd thought it was, the green-eyed radio reporter that I'd last seen on the Headquarters steps, racing late to the Chief's murder conference with her recorder slung over her shoulder. I said, "Yeah, I know you," and I saw her eyebrows go up.

"Did we meet before?" she said.

"No, but we've hung around a lot of the same places. Listen, if it's about the shooting yesterday, I'm not allowed to say anything about it."

"That was you?" she said. "I'm sorry, I didn't know."

"Oh," I said, a little bit disappointed.

"The department didn't release your name yet, they only said that a patrol sergeant was involved."

"Well, do me a favor and don't say it was me that told you. I'm in enough trouble as it is." If it wasn't about that, I was wondering exactly what *was* it that she wanted me for? But then again I didn't want to ask, because that would involve me in some long explanation and I was almost certain that my phone was going to ring in three minutes' time.

"Trouble?" she said. "I thought there was talk of you getting some kind of citation."

"That's half of it. The other half is talk about putting me on a disciplinary charge to cure my delusions of being the avenging angel. But please, that's all I'm going to say."

She said, "But that isn't even why I'm here," and she glanced hopefully over my shoulder into the room beyond. "Can't I just come in for five minutes?"

With eyes like those, I'll bet she was more used to having men run ahead of her to rearrange the furniture so that she wouldn't have to tire herself out zigzagging around too much. But I said, "Maybe we can meet later. I'm expecting an important call on the hour and I don't dare miss it."

"Well," she said, "I won't keep you as long as that," and somehow she'd turned my objection into an invitation and was walking in, and there was I letting her.

Belatedly I said, "Please, this is really too important for me to risk," but she was already setting her bag on the table near the phone.

She said, "Does the name Bobby Winter mean anything to you?"

I was still by the door. I closed it.

"What about him?" I said.

My gun was over in the bedroom on the bedside table, and I'd have to pass her to get to it. I watched her, looking for anything that might betray her as a vessel for the same kind of Trojan-horse trick that had been played with Michaels, but nothing jumped out at me. Could he be *that* good?

She said, "Two kids came into the newsroom yesterday afternoon and told me a story about how a friend of theirs had vanished after a bad crack on the head. They said that a Sergeant Alex Volchak had turned up the next day and told them that he was, quote, on the case. But then when they tried to phone in some new information, they were told that no file had been opened for Winter in the records computer."

"What new information?"

"Somebody saw him on the street and he walked straight past them. I mean someone who knew him well, and he didn't even show a spark of recognition. The way it looks, the kid's not only lost his memory but he's leading a complete new life."

This could be it, I realised, this could be the break in the clouds. He was cocky, he'd been careless. I said, "Where was he seen?" But Angela Price smiled and I realised then that there was going to be yet another kind of price involved here.

She said, "Now wait a minute, Sergeant. Are we agreeing to help each other?"

"Yeah," I said, my mind racing, "I mean . . . look, I need to know," and that was when the phone started to ring.

"There's your call," she said, as if she expected me to break off and take it with her standing there, but I picked up her bag and handed it to her and tried to steer her around and towards the door, saying, "I know, why don't you wait in your car," and she somehow turned it into a neat evasion and left me heading for the door all by myself.

She said, "You just reminded me, I have some pills I have to take. Can I get a glass of water first?"

"In the kitchen," I said, knowing that I was beaten because I simply didn't have the time to mess around. "Help yourself." And as she went through and started to look for a glass, I picked up the phone and turned my back to the kitchen door and wondered if I'd be able to make it so that my end of the conversation wouldn't mean anything if it was overheard.

Winter was there. "Morning, Alex," he said, business-like. "Usual rules, and then I suppose you want to talk."

Which I took to mean that *he* wanted to talk. I said, "Put her on," and he handed over the phone to Georgie.

"Hi, Alex," she said.

"Hello, Georgie. I heard about your mother last night, she's doing fine."

"I know," Georgie said. "He rings the hospital and lets me listen."

"He does?"

"He pretends to be all kinds of people. He can get them to tell him anything."

"Yeah," I said, "I'll bet." Behind me in the kitchen I could hear the distinctive sound of tablets being rattled out of a bottle along with the water being run cold in the basin, so it seemed that this part of Angela Price's excuse had been real, at least. I'd been assuming that it was something they taught them when they went to foot-in-the-door school. I went on, "Here's what I want to know, Georgie. I want you to think back to the day we went to the zoo. Of all the different animals we saw, can you remember which ones you liked best?"

"The monkeys, I guess."

I felt my heart sinking. The possibility that I hadn't wanted to face, that Georgie might have suffered for Winter's frustration and defeat yesterday, rose up before me now.

But then she said, "No, wait, I know what you mean. You're thinking about the baby chicks."

"Yeah, Georgie," I was able to say after a few moments, "that's what I was thinking about."

Angela Price had wandered back through from the kitchen with her glass of water, and she was doing a lousy job of pretending to show an interest in the cheap prints that I'd hung on the walls. Even I don't see that much in them, and I bought the damn things.

But then I had a brainwave, something so simple and so obvious that I wondered why it had taken me until now to come up with it.

I caught her eye, and beckoned her over.

She didn't need asking twice. What she'd overhead so far must have intrigued her, but that was nothing compared to what was on its way. Georgie was saying, "He wants the phone back, now," and so we said goodbye and I waited for Winter to come on the line. I turned the phone slightly, so we'd both be able to hear.

Winter said, "What did you think of the show yesterday, Alex?"

"You ought to be asking those kids, or the woman who got scared half to death."

"This is supposed to bother me? I thought you knew me better than that."

"I know I'm not too impressed by any kind of performance over a safety net like yours. Have you thought over my proposal?"

"You mean, one-to-one at high noon, with all guns blazing? I'll admit that I'm tempted. It's an intriguing scenario."

I could almost hear the cogs and wheels whirring away in Angela Price's mind only inches from me. I was almost afraid that Winter might hear them, too. I said, "Yeah, but you'd cheat. You'd still take out insurance."

"Of course I would," he said. "How else could I have lived so long?"

"You really want to live forever?"

"There is no forever. There's only now."

Angela Price was frowning now. She'd picked up on the antagonism between us, but she was mystified by the details. So in an attempt to steer us onto more accessible ground, I said to Winter, "Let the child go, and face me."

"Sure," he said lightly. "What kind of face would you like to see?"

"How about the Encanto Park killer?"

There was a long silence. Glancing to the side, I could see that Angela Price's eyes were wide-open in surprise . . . and they were shining with a light all of their own.

Winter said, "Are you trying to trace this call?"

"No," I said.

"Never lie to me, Alex," he said. "Just sit back and watch the show, and think about the day when you'll be the star of it. Because that day's coming sooner than you think."

And then he hung up, and after a moment I did the same.

Then I looked at Angela Price and said, "That was Bobby Winter."

She nodded. She walked up and down a little, trying to get it all straight in her mind before we went any further. Winter had suspected me of having the call traced, that was why he'd hung up so fast, which meant that he was ringing from somewhere that he regarded as his base. Somewhere that he wanted to protect, somewhere that he couldn't leave in a hurry.

Somewhere that he kept his insurance, in the form of those empty shells pulled back from the brink of death.

Angela Price said, "What was that about a child?"

"He's holding my neighbor's kid," I said. "You see why I want to find him?"

"And *he's* the Encanto Park killer?"

"He's all messed up. He thinks he's a lot of things. I got onto him and he found out about it, and this is his way of keeping my hands tied. Now do you see why I want to know where he was sighted?"

She took this in, added it to what she already knew. I wanted her to make up her own picture, because she sure as hell wouldn't believe mine.

She said, "Before we go any further. I'm in on this, right?"

"I kind of thought you might want to be. You want to make a deal?"

"Depends on the terms."

"You can follow me around and watch the whole thing," I said, "as long as you don't get in the way and you don't ask questions. You want to try making sense of it, you work it out for yourself."

"Is this the department talking, or just you?"

"The department isn't involved," I said flatly. "This is just me and him."

"Oh, wow," she said, starry-eyed and looking into the distance, but I knew that it wasn't because of me – she was seeing what her report was going to be like when it came out as an exclusive, *I Walked with the Manhunter* or *High Noon in the Valley of the Sun* or some other overblown heap of purple-prose guano.

I said, "I don't care how I come out of this, but we've got to start moving *now*. He's probably planning to hit somebody tonight, that's the show he's talking about – and I don't want to be wasting time looking for those two kids and hauling them out of class, so how about it?"

She dug in her bag, brought out some keys.

"We can go in my car," she said.

25

This suited me fine, as Winter would probably know my car by now. She also wanted me to drive, which suited me as well because I tend to get carsick as a passenger, although I didn't realise the reason behind this request until we'd been on the road for about half an hour. She had me heading south, but wouldn't say exactly where we were going. This was good policy from her point of view, whether she knew it or not, because my intention was to dump her as soon as I had the information I needed. I'd already reported in sick with a phonecall, so from then on my way would be clear.

Ahead of us lay more than a hundred miles of dry cotton-country leading on to Tucson, and beyond that the Mexican border; in between were maybe a dozen small farming towns strung out along the main road, to which I could add homesteads and ranches and a big air base somewhere close to Marana. I'd tried fishing for specifics already, and she hadn't risen to the bait; for my part I was playing it cagy about my own background in the affair, and when she asked me how I'd come to be suspicious of Winter, I said, "I never was. He's the one who picked *me* out with some crazy idea about having met up with me in his other lives. He's about as loopy as they come."

"And you didn't report the kidnap to your superiors?"

"No."

"Do you know what effect this may have on your police career?"

"I'm more concerned with the effect on the little girl," I said, and then something about the style of the questions made me curious and I glanced down and then glanced down again when I realised that I'd just seen that she was holding a microphone and that there was a compact reel-to-reel machine turning on her lap. I said, "How long have you been recording me?"

And she said, "It's what I'm here for. Give me a break, Sergeant. We're en route to foil a kidnap, it's actuality."

"Call me Alex."

"Give me a break, *Alex*."

"Only if you'll tell me where we're going."

She half-smiled then, and looked out of the window. At that moment we were on a long bridge over a dry creek that had tyre tracks on it. She must have decided that we'd come far enough for me not to turn back and set out again alone, because she said, "He was seen in Florence. The University's got a cotton research station or something like that around there, so sometimes the kids out on field studies drop into town to buy stuff. One of them recognised Winter coming out of the general store and saw him climb into a red pickup and drive away, end of story."

"And that's all?"

"It's a start, isn't it?"

"Yeah," I said, although it wasn't as much of a start as I'd been hoping for. Florence was the main town out in Pinal County, not exactly big but certainly big enough for somebody to hide out unseen, especially if they were to base themselves on the outskirts and only come in for essential supplies.

Angela had stopped the tape by now, and she took off the full reel and slipped it into a box which, after she'd marked it, went into the glove compartment. I made sure that I noted where it went. There were some other boxes just like it in there, but most of the space seemed to be taken up by a disorganised private pharmacy.

I found out the reasons for it five minutes later, when she started to sneeze.

I'd been driving along with my window open, as was my habit; but now we were running through wide open fields with ploughed land to the right and cotton to the left, and there was some kind of fine white dust that was lifting and drifting across our path from the planted areas. It was like a dry desert snow, and it seemed to be getting to her. I closed my window, but by then it was too late.

"I moved to the desert because of my asthma," she said apologetically, "so now I have allergies instead. I'm going to have to take something. Just long enough for me to get a glass of water, okay?"

"Sure," I said.

We pulled off the road at a small wooden-hut diner that stood in the middle of a stony clearing on its own. We went in and sat at the counter, and along with the iced water for Angela I ordered a cup of coffee that I didn't want, by way of rent. There was nobody else in the place apart from an older man in a straw stetson at the far end of the counter, who only seemed to be here to talk to the waitress.

When I looked back to see what Angela was doing, she'd taken four or five different bottles out of her bag and was checking the labels on each to see which one she wanted.

I said, "The doctor says you have to take all these?"

"They're not prescription drugs," she said. "They're

164

homeopathic medicines. And before you ask, no, it doesn't mean anything kinky."

"I know what homeopathic means. It means you take a little dose of the same thing that's causing you the problem."

"A renaissance cop," she said cynically. "That's made my day."

"I only said I knew what it meant. That doesn't mean I don't think it's cranky."

"Well," she said, and she unscrewed the cap on the first bottle. It was one of those child-proof ones that only little kids seem to be able to open. "I'm getting to the point where I'm ready to try anything."

"Do they work?"

"Don't ask. Confidence is half the battle."

She took the first couple of pills and chased them down with water, and re-read the label as she waited for them to hit bottom. Swallowing hard like that made her look faintly surprised, as if someone had sneakily peeled the label off and replaced it with a dirty joke.

I said, "I've seen you on crime scenes. I think you're wasted on radio."

"Don't tell me," she said, "tell the people who do the hiring. I've tried to break into TV in three different states, and I still haven't made it. And it's not because I'm no good – it's because of those news consultancies who turn the whole thing into a glamor parade."

"So, where's your problem?"

"I don't want to do the fucking happy-stories, that's my problem."

She picked up the next bottle, and I started to stand.

"Excuse me for one minute," I said. "I just have to go to the washroom."

I ambled down the counter, past the man in the straw stetson who was saying *You can keep all them French painters 'cept Rembrandt*, there's *a guy could paint*, and pushed through a flimsy wooden door marked *Rest Rooms*. As soon as the door had flapped shut behind me I was down to the window at the end of the passageway and climbing out. There was no fenced area or anything, just open land to the back of the diner, and I'd deliberately parked the car around the side so that nobody would be able to see it from the main windows, nobody in this case meaning Angela Price. I was guessing that she'd be up to her third bottle of quack remedies now as I ducked under a back window and skittered around the corner almost on my fingertips, and three long strides covered the rest of the distance to the car.

She was sitting there, ready to go.

"I had the keys with me," she said. "What were you planning to do, hotwire it?"

We rolled into Florence less than half an hour later. It's one of those little towns with a long and lively pioneer history, although at first glance you could be forgiven for thinking that everybody was in the process of moving out so that the buildings could fall down in peace. We slowly cruised down the main street with its covered sidewalks, and Angela spied out the general store with its ten-cents-a-ride rocking horse standing out in the shade. Further along were a Rexell's and a hardware store running a paint sale, but the barbershop and the cinema had closed down and an apartment hotel stood empty. A white Impala was turning ahead of us, and from the Pinal County crest on its door I guessed that the garage and yard set back from the street were for housing the sheriff's vehicles.

"What do we do now?" Angela said. She hadn't mentioned my little breakout bid back at the diner, almost as if she took it to be part of the groundrules of the game.

I said, "I wish I knew. I don't suppose the kids had the number of the pickup."

"No."

"Or the direction it took."

"Out of town, was all they knew."

We circled around the block, and I pulled into a vast and mostly unoccupied parking lot in front of the new county administration building. We'd passed few people on the streets, just a small group of men in checkered shirts and two women in slacks and big-sized print blouses. The town had a real mid-afternoon feel, like there was life around but it was all going on somewhere else.

When I'd stopped the car and turned off the engine, I said to Angela, "Okay, I want you to do something for me," and I brought out the picture of Winter that I'd been keeping by the phone. "Take this over to the store and see if anybody recognises it."

"While you stay here with the car?" she said, with a subtext of *I wasn't born yesterday, buster*.

"If Winter's around," I said, "I don't want him to see me. He could do anything."

She studied the photograph for a while. I realised that this was the first time she'd seen a face to put with the name. She seemed unfazed by Winter's look of innocence, real when the shot was taken but replaced by something more sinister since.

She said, "I'm taking the keys."

"Take one of the wheels, if it makes you feel better."

I watched her as she walked away. I suppose that I was comparing her to Loretta, in the inevitable way that you do. Superficially they were similar in a lot of ways – self-possessed, confident, determined, ready to take knocks without running for cover – but when it really came down to it, Angela Price was of another breed altogether. Newspeople like to put themselves forward as crusaders for the individual, but the fact is that they're really in just another branch of showbusiness. If they can reconcile the two points of view early on, then they've got a reasonable chance of growing old gracefully; but a lot of them don't even think about it, and go striding out with their wooden swords.

I missed Loretta. Missed her sharply, now, and if I couldn't have her back whole I'd have her any way she came. I'd been about to start a new life and Winter had smashed it and scattered the pieces; but I'd put it together again somehow, and when I thought of his true face and his true name I knew that I wouldn't go soft when the time arrived.

I checked the Colt Special in its holster under my jacket, and the spare rounds that I was carrying. And then, remembering that there was something else I had to do, I reached over for the glove compartment; but it was too late, because Angela was walking back across the lot towards me. She was carrying the last two cans from a six-pack of something, using the plastic template as a handle.

She got in beside me, tossing the car keys so I could catch them. "The storekeeper identified the picture," she said, "but you're not going to believe this."

"Try me."

"He bought out their entire stock of baby food. Two boxloads." She studied the effect of her announcement for a moment. "You don't look surprised."

"It's the way my face is made," I said. And then, for appearances, "Why did he want it?"

"He didn't say."

"Did they have an address for him?"

"No, but he placed another order to pick up next week, so he must be staying in the area. So, what now?"

"Give me a minute to think," I said.

"Sure." She popped open one of the soda cans. "You want this? One of them's for you."

"Thanks," I said, "but later."

She shrugged, and started to look through her various bottles of pills again as I wondered about the best way to proceed. Big orders of baby food meant that he had to be maintaining a new group of his zombies, which meant that he had to be somewhere that he could feel safe and unobserved. Hotels and motels would be out, because I'd found him in such places too easily before.

Angela choked on another handful of pills, washing them down with the soda. Watching the face that she made, I said, "Have you ever considered the possibility that you may be a hypochondriac?"

"Wow, doctor," she said, "that sounds really serious, how long does it leave me?"

And then I said, "I've got another idea."

She looked at me suspiciously. "This sounds like you're going to send me out there again."

"Yeah, I know, you're a sick woman. I want you to go over to the county offices and check with the land registry. See if there's any property in the area that's been registered in the name of Michaels."

"Who's Michaels?"

"A businessman whose place he turned over. There were ranch prospectuses and all kinds of things in his office, one of them might have given Winter a line on somewhere local. It's worth a try, anyway. You know who to ask?"

"Please," she said in a pained voice. "I'm a professional."

This time, she didn't even take the keys. I think she was beginning to trust me. I waited as she walked across the plaza to one of the newer county buildings which looked like a big glass-and-sandstone harmonica on its side, and as soon as she'd gone through the main doors I was in the glove compartment and checking through the tape boxes. As soon as I'd found the one with my 'actuality' interview on it, I turned the car radio on loud and held the box up close to the speaker for a couple of minutes so that the working magnets could do their stuff.

When Angela returned, I had everything stowed again.

"I think we're on a winning streak," she said as she climbed into the car, and I could see that she was flushed and eager.

"You found something?"

"An old place out on Highway 89, recently re-registered for development as a turkey farm. They ran me off a copy of the map and everything."

"That's where green eyes get you," I said.

"Don't I know it. They were worth every penny."

"What do you mean?"

"My eyes are brown. These are contact lenses. Listen, Alex, don't you think it's time we went to the authorities?"

I took the xeroxed map that she was offering to me, and said, "Don't take offence at this, Angela, but keep your nose out, okay?"

We were up and running. It could still turn into nothing, but somehow I didn't think that it would.

Highway 89 was a two-lane road running south-east out of Florence, running parallel but some miles east of the main interstate towards Tucson. It didn't take more than two minutes to reach the outskirts of town through the rundown suburbs that spread in all directions from the main street, new or restored buildings standing out here and there like the odd capped tooth. Angela took me at my word, and said nothing for a while.

Out on the highway, I said, "I think I recognise this. We're on the same road where Tom Mix was killed."

"Tom Mix?" she said. "Was he somebody famous?" But she was only doing this to get revenge.

I think she was, anyway.

I slowed down when I thought we were getting close to the place that had been marked on the map, and there it was; an ungated dirt drive with a battered-looking mailbox on a post at its end, the name *Arballo* stencilled on it in faded black letters. A couple of deeper dents in the side suggested that somebody had been using the box for casual target practice. I didn't stop. There wasn't enough cover between the road and the house, a two-story clapboard building which stood about a quarter of a mile back with a new-looking hurricane fence all around it. When I finally did pull in, it was onto a roadside picnic area.

I didn't even have the slightest doubt any more. There had been a red pickup outside the house, within the chain-link compound. I know that red pickups in Arizona are about as rare as flies around a dead horse, but the buildup of the evidence was too persuasive.

I said to Angela, "We have to get him out of the house and away from the child. That's where you come in." And she looked at me with wary suspicion.

"Oh, yeah?" she said.

"All you have to do is go back into town and make a phone call. Make out that you're ringing from the post office and that there's some cash for the farm that's to be collected in person. He'll swallow it, because he needs the money."

"For more baby food?"

"Whatever. As soon as he's hung up, drive back out here with your eyes open for a red truck going in the opposite direction. When you've passed him, put your foot down and get to the farm as fast as you can. I plan to be waiting there with the child."

"*Then* do we go to the authorities?"

"One step at a time, all right?"

She wasn't happy, but the story came first; I was the participant and she was the observer, and all of the moral weight was firmly on my shoulders. I got out of the car so that she could slide over. She could see I knew more than I was telling, especially about the little details like the baby food, but I could always invent something later if she didn't come up with her own explanation first. That's the thing with a psycho killer, anything goes. It's only the psychiatrists who bust a gut trying to make it all fit together, and they always come along after the event.

I walked back to the driveway's end along the opposite side of the road, off the shoulder so that I wouldn't easily be seen from the house. Angela was long gone by the time that I got there, and I crouched down in the scrub to wait. I was sweating already, but I couldn't take off my jacket because then my holster and its hardware would be on show. I didn't know how long this was going to take.

Hunkered down in the dust, I found myself thinking about a frogs' wedding.

It wasn't quite as unlikely as it sounds. The Frogs' Wedding was the first display that Loretta had worked on, and I'd gone along to the mall to look at it one day without telling her. I suppose it was pretty good, of its kind. There was this big fifteen hundred-dollar wedding dress as the centerpiece, and peeping out from under the veil was this frog's face. The groom was a frog, too, in a gray morning-suit and spats. They were surrounded by a half-circle of little frogs, probably because it was too difficult to get a bridesmaid's dress to look convincing on a tadpole. All the frogs were facing outward, champagne glasses raised. To this day I have absolutely no idea what they were supposed to be selling, but I'll bet that they sure as hell didn't move many of the dresses. How many girls dream of looking like Kermit in silk on their wedding day?

But the most important thing had been Loretta's obvious pride in her first piece of work, and that was the reason for it coming back to me now. It hurt like a knife going in. I'd even managed to lose her the display job, along with all the other chaos that I'd brought into her life. I didn't dare mess up again.

The red truck came out after about ten minutes, and I flinched down as it turned within a dozen yards of me. I glimpsed a hard, weatherbeaten face behind the wheel, and felt my first serious twinge of doubt. But it didn't mean anything.

The dust from the truck was still in the air as I started the quarter-mile run towards the house.

26

I kicked in the door and a moment later the smell hit me, and I knew that I hadn't been wrong. It was just like the room in the Paradise Motel, only worse. I stepped in off the front porch, the Special ready in my hand, and waited for my eyes to adjust to the shuttered gloom.

Jesus, he'd been busy.

Four bodies lay in the hallway between me and the stairs, their heads tilted forward and their faces in anonymous shadow, one of them a middle-aged woman with her skirt rucked up around her knees. The man at the end was snoring, gently. And that was only the beginning – when I stepped over them carefully, not wanting to touch anybody, and went through into the sitting room, I came into something that looked like one of those enormous family parties where all the scattered generations come together and then nobody has anything to say to each other. They sat in the chairs and all along the walls, their half-concealed faces grave as if in judgment, their eyes deep and expressionless pits of shadow. I felt as if I'd been left in the wax museum at night, and the doors had been locked, and now the statues had started to breathe. There was Winter, the college kid, sitting with his hand on the phone as if he'd only just put it down. After taking the call, the ghoul had obviously stepped out of him and into the body of the weatherbeaten man. Perhaps he was someone who belonged here, a caretaker maybe, someone who could move around the town without being seen as a stranger. A body too valuable to risk with a bizarre and memorable request like the store's entire stock of baby food.

Winter was the one I shot first.

He bucked once, like dead muscle being touched by a live wire, and then he slumped further forward with the breath rattling out of him. I did each of them the same way, working my way around the room and pausing only to reload as the still-air stink of the bodies gave way to the sharper, irritating smell of cordite. A couple of them bled heavily, but most of them didn't bleed at all. One of them I did sloppily, and made a big mess on the faded wallpaper behind his head. The gun became hotter and hotter in my hand and the air grew thicker in the room, but I made sure of every one of them. Every shot was a story's end.

And then when I climbed the stairs, there were another half-dozen in the bedrooms.

I didn't have enough rounds for them all, and so to save my last load I had to force myself to touch them and to turn them so that their faces were pushed down into the pillows. I pressed on them hard, and they gave in without a whimper. The bedding was cheap and old, like everything else in the house. They talk about atmospheres that you can cut with a knife, but this one you couldn't cut with anything; it would have been like trying to slash your way through a fog, and like a fog it seeped into you and soiled you and left you unclean. I came out of the bedroom checking my watch, wondering how long I had left, and it was then that I caught the sounds of some of the worst recorder playing that I've ever heard.

It was so bad that I couldn't even make out the tune, and I knew that it had to be her. It was coming through muffled from somewhere above, which meant that there had to be a loft or an attic overhead. I wondered how come she hadn't heard the shots or, if she had, why she hadn't reacted. She hardly sounded concerned.

I'd checked all of the bedrooms by now, but I'd overlooked a narrow door which I'd assumed led to a closet but which opened onto an equally narrow ascending stairway. At the top of this was a further solid, six-panel door, and I banged on this and said, "Georgie? Are you in there?"

I didn't get any reply, but the recorder kept on squeaking away on the other side. Didn't even skip a beat, assuming the existence of a beat that could be skipped.

I was wondering how I was going to get a run to break down the door with the stairs just behind me, when I noticed belatedly that the key was in the lock. I opened up and stepped inside.

I got a surprise.

I was expecting the same aura of sleaze that I'd seen in the rest of the house, but the loft appeared to have been cleaned-out and made presentable. Georgie was sitting on the bed and was only just beginning to register wide-eyed astonishment at my unexpected appearance. She was wearing one of those lightweight Walkman headsets and must have been playing along to the music from a cassette, which was why she wouldn't have heard anything. The bedding underneath her was new and so was the T-shirt that she was wearing, a couple of sizes too large and with an 'A' Team logo on the front. She scrambled to her feet, obviously pleased to see me but hesitating slightly, as if she wasn't quite sure whether she knew me well enough to come running over and show it. I went to her and crouched down to her level and took her face in my hands, studying it carefully.

Loretta's eyes looked back at me, giving another twist to the knife.

Georgie said, "Is it okay for me to go home now?" Only she said it too loudly, and I had to reach up and unhook the headset before I replied.

"You bet," I said. "Come on."

"Don't forget Hector. Bobby got him for me."

She was calm and I was shaking, it was ridiculous. I looked around for who or what Hector might be and saw one of those decorated cardboard boxes that pet stores give you to take birds home in, with air-slits cut so that it looks like a little cage. It was standing on the bedside table by her breakfast tray, and I could see that there was something moving around inside.

"A present from Bobby, was he?" I said. 'Well, then, I suppose we'd better not leave him behind." And I went to pick up the box by the cutout loop on the top. I had to step

174

over a video machine and a stack of tapes to get to it; the TV was down at the end of the bed.

"And my new recorder," she said.

"Yeah, your new recorder as well. Listen, I'm going to carry you down and I want you to keep your eyes tight shut, all right?"

"If you mean so I won't see the zombies, I already saw them whenever I came down to the phone."

Something seemed to flip over inside me then, the way it does if you look down and see an unexpectedly long drop. But Georgie seemed completely unruffled, as if the 'zombies' were simply an accepted part of the scenery that wouldn't trouble her any more than the carpets or the wallpaper.

"Well," I said, "just go along with me, anyway," and I gathered her up and got as much of her luggage together as I could carry and then we squeezed out and down the loft stairs to the upper landing. She wasn't heavy, but she was getting just a tad too big to simply scoop up in one arm like a grocery bag. Her face was close to mine so I could see that she was keeping her eyes squeezed shut the way that I'd asked.

As we started down the main stairs to the ground floor, she said, "You forgot my comic books."

"I'll come back later for your comic books. We're in a hurry right now."

"Can I open my eyes yet?"

"Just a minute longer."

"The zombies don't bother me. Bobby explained all that."

"Bobby's full of surprises," I said.

The main door was still half-open from when I'd kicked my way in, and it was letting some much-needed light and air into the hallway. Bobby – the original, at least – was dimly visible way across the sitting room on our left, a discarded glove no longer fit for use. He seemed to be contemplating the powder-stained hole through which I'd stopped his heart for good. An unexpected sliding of tyres on the gravel outside suddenly made me think that I'd allowed my time to run out, but a glimpse of the car through the open doorway told me that it was Angela. I'd have to hurry if she wasn't to see the bodies – the work wasn't finished yet, and a squawk raised too soon might ruin my chances – so I dumped the excess baggage at the foot of the stairs and went out alone with Georgie, pulling the door shut behind me so that Angela wouldn't see the carnage in the hall.

"This is a friend," I said to Georgie in a low voice, "she works for the radio. Don't mention the zombies just yet, okay?"

Georgie, feeling the light on her face at last, opened her eyes and nodded.

Angela was out of her car and coming around. "Is she safe?" she said.

"Great," I told her. "You did a good job."

She opened the door for me so that I could put Georgie into the back of the car. "The pickup went by so fast, I didn't get a look at the driver," she said. "I was hoping that it was him."

"It was," I said. "Let me drive us back, now. There isn't much time."

He was in town now, and I had to find him before he'd had the chance to think too hard about the ruse which had prised him out of his hideaway. I'd succeeded in peeling his disguises from him one by one and now he was down to his last, the weatherbeaten face that I'd glimpsed behind the wheel of the pickup truck, but I'd only keep my advantage if I could get to him before he could realise how vulnerable he now was. The ghoul was there, only one layer of skin deep, and whatever the cost I was going to haul him out into the light to die.

The red pickup was on the street by the post office when we got back into town. I cruised by as slowly as I dared, but I couldn't make out whether he was still inside the building or not. I turned a corner and then parked in the only shade that I could see, and as I started to get out of the car I said to Angela, "Stay with her. Please."

Angela said, "Are you going to the sheriff now?" I could see that she wasn't entirely confident any more, realising that the lines of a news story aren't always so clear when they're seen from the inside.

I said, "Where else?" and tried to smile as if it was all over now as I slammed the door.

As soon as I was out of sight around the corner I started to run, drawing the overworked Special from its holster one more time as I moved. Two dogs in an old picket-fenced garden followed me hopefully from one end to the other, and I could hear their yelping behind me as I crossed the street. This time I wasn't going to hesitate, I'd shoot him out in the open if I had to whether there were witnesses around or not.

But he wasn't in the post office. Nobody was.

Now I had to turn and look around, feeling awkward and conspicuous with the gun in my hand but knowing that I didn't dare have it any other way now that he was so close. I wasn't planning any confrontations or goodbyes, no wrap-up scenes. It would be spy and fire, and I was going to empty the gun into him to be a hundred per cent sure.

Christ, I hoped I could *recognise* him.

But there was no immediate risk of confusion here, because there was nobody else on the street other than me. Down at the far end a Dodge truck was making the turn, pulling a rusty trailer loaded with damp green hay. As it rattled and bumped out of sight I scanned both ways, wondering where he could have gone. Walking distance for him could cover a lot of ground, because I knew how he didn't like to drive if he didn't have to.

The Rexell's, or one of the other stores, maybe? I set off over to check.

I felt a little easier moving under the shade of the covered walkway, a little less conspicuous. Many of the windows along here that hadn't been boarded up carried bars. At the general store I stepped around the kiddy-sized rocking horse in the doorway and followed its cable inside, holding the short-barreled Colt down and out of sight in order not to panic the owner who was rising from a seat behind the counter as I came in.

"Hi," I said, but then I saw the reply die on his lips as his gaze was drawn to one side of me. I reacted, but I was slow. When I turned I saw a rack of free-standing shelves, their contents already beginning to spill as the entire unit toppled towards me; and I was moving, but it was like I was moving through thick grease until the hail of cans passed over me and I was slammed to the floor by a shaky metal structure with all of a big man's weight behind it.

27

I was aware of him crouching over me. I'd lost a minute or so somewhere. Now I was lying on the floor and my head and my shoulder hurt, and a bag of oats had split somewhere so close by that I wanted to cough on the dust.

"Don't shout too soon, Jack," I heard him saying to the storekeeper. "I may have messed up your display, but I just saved you from a robbery."

And then I heard the ignominious sound of a revolver's hammer being cocked just inches from my head. It had to be my gun, because my hand was empty. I heard the storekeeper say, "I guess you did, at that."

Groggily I tried to rise, and cat chow showered from my jacket. He was crouching by me and grinning, a hard-hewn mountain of a man who looked as if he'd been carved from a single chunk of stone with a few uncorrected mistakes along the way. The deadly black O of the Colt hovered before me, but I looked over it and into his eyes. They were the eyes of the ghoul, regardless of the shell that they wore. And the time for playing around, they said to me, was over.

"Wait a minute," a voice said from the doorway, and any hope that I may have had of him being distracted died with the brief flicker of a glance that he spared. I didn't have to look to know that it was Angela, and I didn't know whether to be grateful for this unexpected appearance, or what to feel.

She said, "You're making a terrible mistake." She was

breathless, as if she'd run over. "This man's a police officer working on a kidnap case."

"And who're you?" the ghoul said, his eyes still on me.

"Angela Price, KTAR news. I'm kind of working with the sergeant, here. He was on his way over to see the sheriff."

The weatherbeaten man stood up slowly, my own gun staying on me like a well-trained pointer. I could almost see his mind working, wondering where this new card in the deck might have come from and what she might mean.

And he said, "Well, why don't the three of us go right over there together and sort this thing out?"

"That's the best way," Angela said. She'd never seen this shell before, didn't relate him to Winter, and so saw no reason to worry. She took hold of my arm and helped me to get to my feet, saying, "You took off in entirely the wrong direction, Alex. What did you think you were doing?"

I could have told her, but not in a couple of simple sentences. That would have been all the time I'd have had before we were out on the street again and the big man was suddenly switching the gun from me to Angela, grabbing her by the arm in case she should try to pull away.

"There you go, Alex," he said easily. "I reckon that this way you're less likely to try anything."

Angela looked at me in astonished incomprehension, and then at the man, and then at me again.

"Oh, shit," she said bleakly. "What did I do?"

But I shook my head and briefly raised a hand to show that it was all right. She hadn't known, and couldn't have. And perhaps she'd even bought me a little time – not that I was feeling in much of a state to make good use of it.

"That was a neat piece of business on the phone," the man said. "Now why don't we all get in my truck and then we can go somewhere and talk about this?"

"Who's going to drive?"

"You are. Should I assume that you know the way?"

I walked across the street ahead of them. There was a breeze taking the edge off the sun's glare. He was walking Angela faster than she was really able to go, but she didn't say anything. I got in behind the wheel, and he pushed her in beside me. That way she was between us, and I'd have to reach across her if I wanted to try making a grab at the Colt. It couldn't be done, not even if I'd been feeling sharper and faster than I was now. I was feeling as if I'd had my head inside a big bell for the duration of the twelve o'clock chimes.

I had to force myself into some kind of focus as I started the truck and swung out in a U-turn to head back out of town. As we passed by the general store I could see the owner standing watching us from the doorway, a can of ham in each hand. I couldn't make out his expression because of the shade of the overhang, but I'd have bet that he was wondering what the hell was going on.

The ghoul had noticed it, too, because he looked back through the rear window of the cab and said, "I suppose this means I'm going to have to move out again. But at least I'll know it will be for the last time."

"I wouldn't bet on it," I said, but under the circumstances my bravado sounded distinctly hollow, even to me.

But at least he hadn't got Georgie any more.

The big man sighed happily, and said, "Cocky to the last. I think that's one of the reasons why I'll be so sorry to say goodbye to you, Alex. You've been a pain, but you've made life a lot more interesting than it's been for a long time. I always looked forward to talking to you. I think that's probably what I'll miss the most."

"Think how *I'll* feel," I said. It was weird, listening to him like this. He should have seemed like a total stranger, but in spite of the body and the voice I'd immediately tuned in to the fact that it was the same personality that I'd been dicing and dealing with all along. I couldn't imagine what Angela must be making of it.

He nudged her and said, "See what I mean?" And then he turned his attention back to me. "I was going to tell you all kinds of things," he said. "Stuff that I've never told anyone else. You know that no two people ever see the world quite the same? The shapes and colors are always different, even the sounds. Took me a long time to get the hang of switching. There's a lot more to me than you ever really imagined, Alex. I'm not so stale, and I'm not so stupid, either. I mean, I really fooled you for a while with Michaels, didn't I?"

Michaels.

His body hadn't been anywhere in the house, and I hadn't even thought to notice the fact. Not even up in Georgie's loft, when I'd had to step over the video recorder that had most probably been looted from his den. I'd been starting to wonder whether I'd have the nerve, if a suitably big truck should appear heading toward us in the other lane, to swing us across into its path; but with a zombie still in reserve somewhere, it would be a wasted sacrifice. The bird would fly, the cycle would start again.

As it always had.

I said, "I can't listen to much more of this. Why don't you kill me here, and get it over with?"

"I wasn't planning to *kill* you," he said, making himself comfortable in the angle between the seat and the door. He was too far away for me to reach. "I've got a much better use for you than that."

I was turning from the highway onto the dirt drive when she did it, impulsively and without any warning; she grabbed at the wheel and gave it a hard wrench so that it spun out of my hands, and the pickup suddenly veered over to the right. I could see the mailbox coming, but I couldn't correct in time; the front of the truck simply smashed the post from under it as if it was so much matchwood, while the box bounced once on the hood and came straight up through the windshield and into the cab. I lost it completely then, because Angela had thrown herself over against me and the truck was onto the rugged ground beyond the shoulder, but I could see the mailbox behind her jammed into the cab at an angle like an unexploded rocket. Then we must have hit an even deeper rut, because the nose of the truck dropped violently and I felt myself being pitched forward; and that was all that I knew for a while, until Angela was shaking me awake and I opened my eyes to that fierce and painful desert sky.

I was out of the truck, and flat on my back. I struggled up onto my elbows and said, "Where did he go?"

"He's a mess, Alex," Angela said. Her face was marked

with little flecks of blood, probably flying cuts from the imploding windshield. "His head's all messed up, he won't get far."

"Which way?" I said.

"Up toward the house." She tried to hold me down. "What are you doing?"

"Got to finish it," I said.

"Alex!" she insisted as I managed to get on the move, seeing the house an impossible distance away across the field before me, "For God's sake, let's go and get some help! The little girl's safe back in my car!"

"Nobody's safe," I said as I stumbled onto the dirt road that we'd left, but I don't think she heard.

About twenty yards further on I found my gun, lying where he'd dropped it. There was a gory smear on the ground close by, so perhaps he'd fallen. He had to be in quite a state, because he'd been right in the path of the mailbox. But thank God it hadn't quite killed him. I picked up the Colt and, with my other hand, wiped my eyes. I was feeling better, or I was kidding myself that I did; either way, I now felt more able to go on.

"Alex," Angela said from beside me, "you hardly know what you're doing. I'm coming in with you."

"Whatever you like," I said. "But don't interfere."

And she didn't; she stayed just behind my shoulder as we walked up to the front of the house and stopped under its blind, shuttered gaze. It must have looked good at one time, almost colonial, but someone had been letting it go for at least ten years, possibly more. The shape of the Colt was now feeling strange in my hand, as if it had been charged with the lives that it had taken and was hungry for more. How many, now? I'd actually lost count . . . but in a way it was none of my business, it was something between the gun and the ghoul, and I was simply a hapless intermediary who happened to have walked off the street and into the Paradise at the wrong time.

The main door of the house was now half-open, and I had a definite memory of pulling it closed behind me so that Angela wouldn't see the bodies inside. Well, she was going to see them now.

"Holy Jesus Christ on a bicycle," I heard her say from

the threshold behind me as I stood in the middle of the twilit hall and looked around.

"There's plenty more where they came from," I said, waving her toward the sitting room as I tried to work out which way he'd gone from here. Not up the stairs, because the stuff of Georgie's that I'd dropped off at the bottom was undisturbed. Angela picked her way past me, stepping over the stick-legs of the outstretched dead like someone crossing subway rails, and put her head into the sitting-room. There was no arguing with it, she had nerve. I heard her breathe some expression of shock, but didn't make out what it was.

My guess was that he was making for the inert body of Michaels, his last refuge, but I couldn't think where he might have been keeping it. I'd searched the house pretty thoroughly, all the rooms and the cupboards and the closets, and if there had been any evidence of a cellar I'd have searched that, too.

"You already knew about this," Angela said. "And you didn't tell me!"

"I was saving the best for the last," I said. I'd seen a bloody smudge just by the handle of the door which led through into the kitchen, so now I went over and, with the Colt at the ready, gave it a gentle push. It swung open onto a shaft of daylight, bumping on something behind. The far door of the kitchen, which gave out onto the back of the house, had been thrown wide. The heads of the four small bodies which lay under the table were only just into the light.

Angela said, with just a faint trace of shame that she'd probably get over, "Do you think I can get away with using the phone?"

"Try it and see," I said.

I wasn't entirely unhappy that she was along, providing that she didn't get in the way. Right now her mind was probably racing, taking in this new information and hammering it out into a pattern which would include Bobby Winter and the man in the pickup and which would make more sense to an outsider than anything that I could invent. As for me, I only had one thing on my mind. I crossed the kitchen and went to take a look out the back.

And there he was.

He was down in the dust and making about three yards a minute at his current speed. He'd lost the use of his legs now and was scrabbling along like some badly chopped-about worm with a definite destination in mind. Ahead of him lay a big ramshackle barn or garage with a couple of outhouses tacked onto its sides, but he still had a way to go before he got there. In all my career, I don't think I've ever seen anyone so badly injured. A good piece of his head had to be missing.

I could hear Angela dialling when I stepped back into the house, and knew that she'd be tied up for a few minutes at least. At the foot of the stairs I picked up Georgie's pet-store box and said, "C'mon, Hector, I've got a little job for you," and the bird inside scuttled around a little. He didn't have much space in the box, but she'd probably let him out to fly around the room. When I returned to the outside the ghoul had put on a spurt and covered half of the remaining distance to the barn, but the futility of his best efforts must have been apparent to him as I overtook him and, with a show of what must have looked like sadistic courtesy, swung out the barn doors.

It was then that I saw that he hadn't only been stockpiling bodies, but vehicles as well; there were five cars crammed tightly into the big shed, and foremost amongst them was a white police department St Regis, unmarked.

Michaels was in the driving seat with his head back against the rest, looking as if he'd dozed off on duty.

So this was the ghoul's hole card, set up and ready for a getaway. I set the bird-box on its hood and looked in each of the other cars, but this was the only one with an occupant. The others looked as if they'd taken a few bumps and scrapes as he was hiding them away; the dents showed up as new scars except on Winter's Toyota, the one he'd called Joshua, where they simply blended in.

I turned to the ghoul. He seemed to have given up on the last few feet and had simply rolled over, exhausted, to rest with what was left of his head propped against the open barn door. The windshield glass appeared to have flayed most of his face away so that he'd actually come to resemble the image of malleable clay that I'd tried to create in my mind.

184

As I was opening the driver's door of the St Regis, I said, "I suppose you realise that this was a bad move. You should have kept him in another place, another town altogether. But then, I can imagine how I scared you out of the idea of making another long journey the last time we did this."

And then I crouched down and put my arm around Michaels' shoulders, and tipped him forward so that his head bent over the wheel. A few seconds passed, and then I could feel him shudder as he began the final stage of the drawn-out death process.

The ghoul was watching me with his one, bloody, murderous eye, too weak to interfere and too hurt to make the leap unaided. He was like a man at the deck rail of a burning ship, watching the last of the lifeboats pulling away. Michaels was shivering hard now and I kept my arm around him, using his throes to help me resist any temptation to pity that I might feel for this broken creature on the ground before me. I had to remind myself that this mutilated shell was no more than a temporary habitation and that within seconds, given the chance, he'd be coming at me in another frame madder than any dog.

When Michaels was gone I gave his shoulder a final squeeze and then eased him back in the seat. From over by the door I heard a despairing groan, the first sound of any kind that the ghoul had made in the last ten minutes or so. I went and knelt down beside him and he looked at me, his eye a tiny pinpoint of fury that he hadn't the strength to express.

So here we were, one-to-one, and at last the ghoul lay naked and defenceless.

I said, "You've made me do things a man should never have to do. I've seen things that no-one should ever have to see." And as I spoke I was putting the Colt into his hand, smearing my prints to replace them with his own; and even as I was doing this he was weakly but gamely trying to pull the trigger on me, and the hammer fell on an empty chamber exactly as I'd set it. When I let go of his hand, it fell by his side. He didn't even have the strength to raise it again.

I thought he had maybe a couple of minutes longer, if he

was lucky. It took everything he had to manage at last a faint, hoarse whisper.

He said, "*No, Alex. Not this. Not to me.*"

Perhaps it was the way he used my name, I don't know, but I felt a tug of something inside. Something that I knew I didn't dare pay much attention to. I said, "I know, you're a strange and wonderful thing. But you never took a step without walking on somebody."

"*I didn't hurt the child.*"

"No. But you would have, in the end."

The glimmer in his dying eye told me that I'd spoken the truth, and that both of us knew it.

I leaned closer.

"I could end it for you here," I said. "But there's something I want you to understand before you go."

28

When Angela Price came out a few minutes later, the farm caretaker lay dead with my untraceable Colt Special in his hand. For anybody who wanted to work it out, it would look as if he'd committed mass slaughter in the house and then crawled over here with the notion of escaping in one of the cars. That didn't leave me exactly free and clear, but it took me a lot of the way.

I looked up from beside him and said to Angela, "Did you call the sheriff?"

She looked once at the body beside me, and then looked away again. None of the dead inside the house had been quite as messy as this, and what had been the ghoul was also lying out in full daylight. She said, "Right after I called the network. There's a news crew on its way down here in a helicopter."

Yeah, I could bet on it. I could also bet that she'd spent at least half of the time negotiating a television contract for herself before she'd disclosed the location of the story. Straightening up and dusting myself off, I said, "Well, I'm going to disappear."

Her eyes widened. "What?" she said. "You can't!"

"Only for as long as it takes to get Georgie to her mother. Tell the sheriff I'll be turning around and coming straight back, and then I'll tell him anything he wants to know."

"He won't like it."

"You're right, he won't."

And I probably didn't have much time before he'd get here. I picked up the bird box from the hood of the St Regis and took it around to the Toyota, which was the only other car that could be rolled out of the barn without a lot of maneuvering. The engine turned over easily and started on the third try. Angela followed me out around the side of the house, and in the rearview mirror I could see her standing at the top of the drive as she watched me go. She probably didn't want to go back in the house alone, and I couldn't blame her. Before I turned out onto the main road I checked in my mirror again, only now she was shading her eyes and watching the sky.

The bird in its pet store box was on the passenger seat now. I'd held it in place with the seat belt, otherwise it would have slid around every time I hit the brakes. As the outskirts of the town approached, I could hear it tearing at the cardboard from the inside.

"Either you stop that," I said, "or I tape over the airholes."

That quietened him for a while.

Georgie was asleep on the back seat of Angela's car when I got there, but she woke up as I was carrying her over. I'd decided to stick with the Toyota, which seemed to be fine apart from a tendency to jump out of gear on a stop. Georgie sat in the back, yawning and blinking as I drove another two blocks in search of a pay phone; I saw a lot of activity around the county sheriff's compound, in addition to the three cars that had passed me at speed on their way out to the farm. From the phone I rang Loretta's number, and left a message on Heilbron's answering machine. His taped message said that he was at the hospital, so that would be where I'd go. When I got back to the car Georgie was leaning forward on the back of the passenger seat so that she could look over at the bird box, and she was frowning. But she didn't say anything, and dropped back as we moved out.

I took no chances on the way back, no speeding or anything, and just before we reached the city outskirts I turned off down a sideroad. Once out of sight of the rest of the traffic I stopped. I walked off the track for about two hundred yards, and there after wiping my leather holster I scraped a hole in the dust and buried it. Looking back as I returned to the car, I found that it was already impossible to say where the hole might be.

Georgie seemed to be holding up pretty well. She certainly wasn't the distressed wreck that I might have expected her to be after a week as a captive and in strange company. When we were moving again, I said, "How did he treat you?"

"He was okay," she said, coming forward to lean on the back of the passenger seat again. She could barely reach to see over. "He was explaining stuff *all* the time. Like he'd never had anyone to talk to before."

"What kind of things did he say?"

"Weird stuff," she said, and when I glanced at her I don't think I'd ever seen a kid looking so thoughtful, and so troubled. I asked her to tell me what kind of 'weird stuff'.

So she told me about how he never slept if he could help it; how when a body grew tired he'd move to another, even if it was only for a few hours. She'd asked him why and it had emerged that he was terrified by his own dreams. He'd told her about another time when he'd been forced to take refuge in a bedridden soldier who'd been so sick and so feverish that he'd been unable to get out again until almost a year later, when a nurse had come along at four o'clock on a Christmas morning and injected him with a massive dose of morphine, silent tears silvering her face in the moonlight. He'd said that food had no taste for him, but that every life tasted different. He'd said that young life gave him a hit like cocaine. Georgie thought that he'd meant like Space Dust, only stronger, and I didn't try to explain it to her. Apparently she'd quickly begun to recognise him through whatever mask he was wearing when he came up to her loft with some new comic books or a TV Guide or some piece of loot that he'd thought she might like; she'd told him that she always knew him because of his eyes. Whoever he was in, she'd said, his eyes were always sad.

Then he'd said that he could try to teach her the trick of it, if she wanted; that maybe she could do it if he came along with her and prepared the way, and maybe then they could get around and have some real fun and never have to worry about being caught.

I looked sideways at her, quickly; she was still leaning forward, staring down at the bird box over the back of the passenger seat. "What did you say to that?" I asked her.

"I told him no thanks," she said, and she stretched over as far as she could and reached down to put her finger to one of the slots in the box. The reaction was instantaneous, a squawking and a fluttering which caused her to pull away so fast that she teetered for a moment before dropping back onto her seat. I glanced in the mirror at her as she added, "I mean, who'd want to end up being like *him*?"

It was almost five in the afternoon when I pulled onto the parking lot outside the Phoenix Zoo. I told Georgie that I had a quick visit to make and that I wouldn't be more than a few minutes, and then I unbelted the bird box.

And as I was lifting it out, Georgie said, "You trapped him in Hector, didn't you?"

I stopped, half-in and half out of the car. I could see from her face that there was no point in me trying to make up some lie, so I said, "I'm afraid I did. I made it so he had nowhere else he could go." I didn't want to tell her about how I'd carefully squeezed the life out of the bird to bring it right up to the point of death and no further, or about what I'd had to do to the body of the farm caretaker to drive the ghoul across.

"Is he going to die?" she said. "I mean, for real, this time?"

"Yes," I said. "He is."

She thought about it for a few moments. Then she nodded.

"I think it's best," she said. "That's what he wants, really."

The zoo was about to close and the girl at the turnstile wasn't going to let me in, but I said that I was here to see one of the assistant managers and mentioned Frank's name. She must have phoned ahead, because as I walked towards the Administration block over by Macaw Island I saw him coming out to meet me. He gave me a friendly enough hello, but I could see that he was puzzled at my appearance so late in the day and I also saw his eyes stray to the box under my arm.

I explained what I wanted, making it sound casual and nothing special. He shrugged, and went over to call something into one of the offices, and then together we walked down the path that would take us out to the eastern spur of the grassland habitat area. Where two paths crossed, we stopped to let the last Safari Train of the day go by.

I hadn't been consciously trying to think of the last time that I'd been here but the memory was with me all the same, trotting along at my side like some faithful old dog. Frank, who knew nothing of what I'd been through in the past few weeks, was saying, "You should hear some of the things we get asked. Weird? We had a woman six months ago, wanted to buy some gorilla semen. I don't even like to *think* about why."

"Did she get it?"

"We told her that she could have as much as she wanted, but she'd have to do her own collecting. What the hell, you've seen our gorilla, he needs all the fun that comes his way. She didn't ring back. What did she think, that we kept it around in bottles?"

Here on our left was the drinking fountain where we'd stopped before leaving. Georgie hadn't been able to reach, or so she'd said. So I'd lifted her to it, and she'd managed to spray both Loretta and me.

Frank said, "All I'm wondering is, what did the bird do to offend you so much?"

"Not me," I said. "It's my nephew's. It got a taste for blood."

"A *canary*?"

"It must have seen too many Sylvester cartoons. Now there's no stopping it. This is the best way."

The final bell was ringing as we reached the line of pens which held the birds of prey.

Frank called a keeper out from around the back, and he produced the keys to open up the walk-through feeding alley by the side of the hawks. There were three of them, sleek, well-oiled machines with dark little hearts, and at the noise we made they turned and stared at us from their perches with eyes that were like small, beady lasers. They kept on staring as I put my box through the hatch and opened up the lid.

Within an instant there was a sharp pain in my hand as the canary came out in a flurry of yellow feathers, and it struggled and fluttered as I tried to shake it off. Frank and the keeper were both staring in surprise at the quarter-inch gash that its beak left in my hand, so deep that the blood simply ran, but I only had eyes for the birds.

The canary was zigzagging around, completely disoriented after its time in the box. Two of the hawks had already started to move, Indian sun-gods with their cloaks spread wide, and I drew my bleeding hand back and let the wire hatch fall shut.

"You could have released it," Frank said. "Cage birds hardly ever make it in the wild anyway."

"I want to be sure of this one," I said. "And I want him to know what it felt like for the rest of us."

It lasted no longer than a single wing-beat, of which I could feel the backdraft like the passage of a dark angel. The yellow bird was picked from the air with a squawk and returned to the perch, where the biggest of the hawks held it and decapitated it. After that, there was no sound other than that of tearing and feeding.

I told Frank that I owed him one.

And then I headed back toward the car, where Georgina would be waiting.

MORE TITLES AVAILABLE FROM NEL